Conway Moncure

A Necklace of Stories

Conway Moncure

A Necklace of Stories

ISBN/EAN: 9783337149925

Printed in Europe, USA, Canada, Australia, Japan

Cover: Foto ©Andreas Hilbeck / pixelio.de

More available books at **www.hansebooks.com**

'Tis said the necklace grew from iron chain ;
Strength by that transmutation was its gain :
Best truth is weak that starts free hearts' alarms,
They only are restrained whose chains are charms.

A

NECKLACE OF STORIES

BY

MONCURE D. CONWAY

WITH ILLUSTRATIONS BY W. J. HENNESSY

London

CHATTO AND WINDUS, PICCADILLY

1880

Printed by R. & R. CLARK, *Edinburgh.*

CONTENTS

LIST OF ILLUSTRATIONS

THE INVISIBLE QUEEN

THE INVISIBLE QUEEN.

In the year 1587 Sir Walter Raleigh fitted out three vessels for an expedition to reinforce a colony which two years before had settled on the island of Roanoke, on the coast of what was then known as Virginia. When these ships arrived, they found the colony deserted, the bones of the settlers scattered on the beach, and wild creatures crouching in the ruins of their habitations. Having repaired the houses as well as they could, the new colony remained in the island. On the 18th of August in the same year, Eleanor, wife of Councilman Dare, and daughter of Governor White, gave birth to a daughter. This was the first white child born in America, and she was named Virginia. Nine days after her birth, Governor White sailed for England to procure supplies, leaving on the island eighty-nine men, seventeen women, and eleven children. He directed the settlers that if they should abandon Roanoke, they were to carve upon some conspicuous object the name of the place to which they migrated, and if they went away in distress, a cross should be carved above the name.

When White reached England, he found the country in wild excitement about the threatened invasion of the Spanish Armada, and it was nearly three years before he could procure the supplies and sail with any safety for Virginia. When at length he landed at Roanoke, not one of the colonists he had left there could be found. The houses were in ruins, their goods were found scattered or buried. A fort had been erected, and within this was found marked on a post— though without any cross, which indeed was not needed—the single word CROATOAN.

From that day to the present no tidings have ever come from any member of that colony.

Speculations have been rife, and a number of Indians once found in that region, of somewhat lighter complexion than other tribes, gave rise to a tradition that the Roanoke settlers had been absorbed. In the course of two centuries it even became a sign of family antiquity among the Virginians if any tint of the Indian complexion appeared in their line. The following story, however, which has lately reached me, suggests that the lost colony had issues even happier than the charms of Southern brunettes or the chivalry of their brothers.

About the time when a happy girl was suddenly summoned to the throne of England, where she still reigns as Victoria, seven young Englishmen found themselves together in Cuba. One was a poet fresh from Oxford; two were youthful noblemen in search of adventure; two were artists; the two others were students of science, who had been examining the coral reefs of that region. These agreed together to pass a

month or more in excursions along the eastern
coast of America. So they purchased a pretty
yacht, "The Fancy," and first sailed to Florida.
They penetrated far inland, and when after some
days they returned to their yacht, the savants had
rare flowers and minerals, the artists their sketches,
and the poet a romance showing that he had come
nearer finding El Dorado and its enchanted
fountain than either De Leon or De Soto who
had so long sought the same in that region.
They then sailed northward. After some days,
they hardly noted how many, a strong westward
wind struck the sail of the "Fancy," and, though the
sky was cloudless, their hands found it hard as any
storm to struggle against. " Well," said the English
youths, " do not struggle against it ; let us go westward, fancy-free." The prow turned, the " Fancy"
sped like an arrow to Ocracock Inlet, and when
she had got behind the long bar that fringes the
Carolina coast, became as docile as a child ought
to be while reading this story. They passed on

northwards, until they came to a beautiful wooded island. As they approached this they beheld a charming scene. On the yellow sands of a long beach, graceful Indian women and children were gathering shells ; some were sporting amid the bright waves, and from the merry groups peals of laughter came out to them over the water. " Let us land!" cried six voices of the " Fancy" in chorus ; but the seventh, the poet, said, " Beware ! it is the island of Circe!" This was the poet—who was the first to land.

The islanders came running from their beach—there were only maidens and children—and with smiling kindly faces they formed a circle round our voyagers, hand clasped in hand. They then began to urge them towards the interior of the island. This reminded the poet of Circe again, but his suggestion was less formidable than that of another of the party who had read that the Sinhalese savages used to decoy mariners to destruction by means of such nymphs. The young noblemen and the artists appeared quite satisfied to incur any fate their merry captors might provide for them; the others made an attempt to break through the circle, but the Indian women were vigorous as they were gentle, and the surprised youths found themselves merrily restored to the ring. During all this play no word was spoken by the Indians. When the procession had gone about a mile from the beach, it halted beside a high rock. The women then proceeded to tie the hands and bandage the eyes of their dismayed captives; after which they marched forward again for what all agreed was at least one hour, and the noblemen always affirmed to be twelve. During the march there was still much mirth among their captors, which was all our adventurers had to reassure their misgiving spirits.

When at last they halted again, the bandages were removed. They found themselves on the street of a little city so beautiful, that at once all fear left them. Not in such a realm could

savagery dwell. There were, indeed, in the archi-
tectural styles of the houses some survivals of
the primitive log-cabin, and even of the wigwam ;
but the logs were selected from a large variety of
trees, the grain of each wood brought out by
finest polish, and the colours exquisitely har-
monised in each home and public edifice. With
the many-coloured woods of the buildings there
were marbles of various tints used about door-
ways and windows with perfect taste. The re-
sidences were all marked by some individuality ;
each had its charming garden, in which young
persons of both sexes, in slight but picturesque
garb, were pleasantly engaged watering flowers
or trimming fruit-trees. Some of these caught
sight of the Europeans passing, and such hastened
to throw open their garden gates, and in clear
English speech invited the captors and captured
to enter. Now and then the invitation was
accepted, and the foreign party enjoyed oppor-
tunities of seeing the interiors of these pretty

mansions. These enhanced their wonder and admiration. They passed through airy halls, adorned with statuary, into rooms whose floors were bordered with lace-work of many-coloured wood, and sometimes partly covered with carpets woven of many-hued grasses, or again adorned with striped and spotted skins of animals. These last, indeed, were in some instances hung up as tapestries, and fringed with brilliant feathers. The European artists were nearly beside themselves with delight. For the rest the pleasure was enhanced by the continual offer of fruits, such as bananas, figs, fox-grapes, peaches, also chinquepins, and beverages light and cool, never stimulating; above all, by the increasing evidences that they were among a tribe kindly as it was happy.

The feeling of fear in the Europeans had given way to emotions of admiration, and now these, in turn, were being merged in a curiosity which grew all the stronger that it did not appear to be reciprocated by the citizens, who, though they gathered around, asked them no questions. One of the men of science could not repress his desire for more light, and asked the smiling dame at his side, " Do you generally, that is to say often, bring foreign folks in this way, eyes bandaged, and so forth ? "   " Not so often as we should like," replied she ; " many sails draw near our beach, where we often sport in the summer time, but after hovering near for a little, they flit away again, they do not land."   " But why did you capture, that is, take possession of us when we landed ? "   " There is a tradition among us that many generations ago our tribe dealt cruelly by a company of pale-faced men and women who landed among them ; they thought them demons, and so treated them ; that tradition is now a grief to us, and we long to bring such among us that we may be kind to them, and may show our gratitude for their having been the means, even when our fathers slew them, of leaving with us a priceless benefit which we still enjoy."

This last reply completely puzzled the Europeans, and was followed by question after question ; but the Indian lady put her finger on her lips, and pointed to a group of little girls who came running to meet them. These little Indians, with the utmost confidence, approached the Europeans, each offering to the one whose hand she took a flower and a kiss, saying, "We are sent to lead you to the palace."

This palace, at which they all presently arrived, was circular, built of purest white marble, and crowned the summit of a wooded hill. Ascending this hill and then a long winding stairway, they entered, and found themselves in a beautiful room and in the presence of a hundred or more Indians, of both sexes. The tapestries of this room were formed of skins of animals artistically combined, and bordered with plumage of rare birds; and there were many decorations of graceful antlers and flowers. Strange to say, there were also some well-painted portraits on the walls. On a throne

sat a handsome youth, and great was their surprise
to hear him addressed, in English, as the Queen of
Croatoan. Another thing made them wonder :
although all the natives around him so quaintly
called Queen had swarthy complexions and straight
black hair, the youthful prince himself was painted
blonde, and his head was covered with a wig of
luxuriant female hair, of golden tint, from which
long and beautiful curls fell upon his shoulders.
On a shelf just over him rested a golden crown,
but at no time did the king wear it.

One of the young women advanced, and still
speaking in English, told the "Queen" the
circumstances under which they had brought
these men. The man-queen then addressed them,
and said they were quite welcome and need not
fear. They should, he said, be hospitably enter-
tained so long as they chose to remain, and the
only condition on which the tribe insisted was,
that when they went away, it should be as they
came,—with bandaged eyes. He then ordered

refreshments, and when the rest had been dismissed, sat down with them. He bade them ask him any questions they might wish.

Fully reassured, the Englishmen were burning with curiosity about many things; insomuch that when the king-queen had invited questions, they all broke out at once, their voices drowning each. other. At this his Majesty laughingly told them it was the custom of Croatoan that deputations to the Court should consult together beforehand as to the precedence of their questions and demands, and he advised them to adopt the same plan. This they did, and the questions of the seven were put one after the other, as follows :—

"What is the origin and history of this tribe ?"

" How do they happen to speak English ?"

"Why is your Majesty, being a young man, called a Queen ?"

"Why does your Majesty wear a woman's hair ?"

" All about your Majesty's wig ?"

"Who painted these pictures, including your Majesty's face?"

"Why must we come and go blindfold?"

The man-queen having taken a note of each question, replied:—"Of the questions you have asked I will first partly answer the last. There is but one weapon of defence that we have ever found it necessary to use against other races and tribes, that is, to provide that they do not see the paths by which they enter our happy valley. As to the other questions, they will all be answered by a narrative which will require your patience.

"It is the tradition of our tribe that their fathers dwelt in a beautiful country, where they were peaceful and happy, until one day a number of white demons attacked their stores. These they were able to destroy; but they then became very uneasy, and the land, which before seemed enchanted, was now haunted with terrors. While exploring in the direction from which the supposed demons had come, they came upon their settlement, and those who had remained in it were slain—all save two. Inside the fort they found a young woman weeping while she tenderly pressed to her breast a beautiful babe. At this sight of the snow-white babe drawing life from its fair mother's breast, our warriors paused. The chief took the child in his arms; the mother fell down and clasped his knees; the babe smiled in his face and played with the shells of his necklace. Amid the ruins of that fort a council was held, and although the warriors were victorious, they determined to leave the retreat, which had been discovered by their enemies, and where some of their best men had been slain. It was no longer to them CROATOAN, the Land of Peace. The cry was raised for another CROATOAN. They looked with pity on the white mother and her babe, and made signs to her to follow them. She gathered up some little treasures that lay around her, and presently came forth with the child in her arms.

"Our fathers then wandered to another coast, made themselves rafts, and reached this island. The fair mother and her babe were kindly cared for. She had brought with her some books and trinkets. In the course of time she revealed and taught to our tribe a wonderful art. She painted the first pictures we ever saw, and instructed some of our youth in the arts of which you see the effects around you. She also began the work of teaching us a better language than our own, and it is her language we now speak.

"But if our tribe honoured and protected the mother, until at length she seemed to forget the sad past and to find joy in our ways of life, what shall I say of her daughter as she advanced in years? Look at this picture!"

The man-queen drew a string : a curtain was drawn back from a picture just above the golden crown, as that was above the throne. Then he bent his head low down, and for a few moments seemed to be engaged in silent worship. The

Europeans could not repress a cry of astonishment. They beheld the life-sized portrait of an English maiden, surpassingly beautiful. It was of half length; about the graceful neck and arms were ornaments which, though barbaric, were evidently the finest that any tribe could have secured, and they were arranged with exquisite taste. Above these rose a face full of noble beauty and refined expression, full also of happiness. The clear blue eyes seemed to the Europeans to beam upon them with a glad surprise, and with welcome; and yet it was with a serene look that said, "I have taken a sweet draught from that magical fountain of which old voyagers dreamed, and no vision of past or future overshadows my earthly paradise."

There was something about the picture which struck the Europeans with a sense of having somewhere seen it a few moments before. This puzzled them, but it was explained as soon as the man-queen again spoke: when they turned to look at him they saw, with smiles hardly to be suppressed, that his curious make-up was meant to resemble, as nearly as possible, the portrait of the maiden on the wall!

"Her mother called her Virginia," continued the royal speaker, "and Virgin she remained; but to our tribe she was known only as the Queen of Croatoan. Before her day they had been ruled by chiefs; but as she grew in beauty and wisdom, as she taught them her mother's language, and brought to bear upon every man, woman, and child, a gentle influence that made them pure and happy, there fell upon all our people, as it were, some inspiration; they built this palace in which you sit, and made a throne, and bore her hither upon it to be their Queen.

"From generation to generation it has been handed down that she lived a hundred years. From the time that she sat, while yet hardly more than a girl, upon this throne, our tribe knew no crime, or wrong, or grief. Between the cry of birth and the sigh of death our simple people lived in a peace and harmony, a health and purity, which realised the ancient dream of their ances- tors—CROATOAN.   It was also the Land of Gold, because their deep Content turned all to gold ; it held the fountain of Youth, for happy hearts are ever young.   There were no taxes laid upon the tribe, for they needed neither prisons nor defences. As for supporting the Queen and her aged mother, it was rather they who supported the tribe, by teaching them how to find in the earth itself a mother's breast and father's bounty.

"When her mother died, she left to the tribe that picture of her daughter.   None ever dreamed of marrying the beautiful Queen, for she was espoused to the invisible genius of the tribe.   But as time passed by, the Queen grew aged, and in her feebleness she called to her aid two of those whose fathers had once led the tribe ; through them she sent, from time to time, her messages and gifts to all.   Sometimes then she was carried

about in a chair with wheels—her own invention
—that she might converse with her people ; and
for the children, who were held up to receive her
kiss, the memory of it was a richer bequest than
gold. But at last these her appearances in person became rare, and finally ceased. Yet every
day the people assembled at the palace to receive, through her ministers, messages from their
Queen, and to return to her expressions of their
constant devotion.

" This went on for a long, long time. That
the Queen should live so long presently seemed
wonderful ; at length, when those who had known
her in girlhood had died, this continued existence
was felt to be miraculous. Her birthday was
well known, and its return was always celebrated
with festivities. The hundredth day from that
birth dawned, and yet it found the tribe in front
of the palace still listening to greetings sent out
from their Queen !

" After a time one of her ministers died, and

the other brought word that the Queen desired no
other to be appointed in his place.   Presently the
remaining one also drew near to death, and, having called to his bedside his own son, he consulted
with him.   He then announced that the Queen
had desired this son of his to be her only minister; and, since to our tribe her wish was always
law, no one dreamed of questioning this arrange-
ment.   When this young man's father had died,
and he had been installed in the palace, a wonderful message was by him brought to the people
from their Queen.   She said that in the night a
being had appeared to her, and announced that
she should never die so long as her people loved
and trusted her; but that this love and trust must
be shown by her subjects, in bringing every month
some offering to the door of the palace.   This was
cheerfully done by all.   And now there grew among
the people an awe concerning their Invisible
Queen.   One and another remembered strange
legends about her infancy, about her apparition

to the tribe surrounded by 'demons,' brandishing flames, and on all sides were the proofs and products of her supernatural wisdom. Little by little the now Invisible Queen was, in the faith of our tribe, transformed to a goddess. Every return of the birthday that found her yet alive, after the limits even of lives legendary in our tribe were passed, confirmed this faith, and made it a conviction so strong, that in every house was built a shrine to her. The arts our tribe had learned from her mother and herself were never lost, and now the picture was copied, and copies multiplied, so that one was hung over each shrine. On her shrines were written these words :—VIRGINIA, THE STAR OF CROATOAN.

"Another minister came, appointed by the previous one, who expired. This new minister brought from the Invisible Queen a message that the spirit had again appeared to her, and told her that her immortality, depending though it did on the love and trust of her subjects, was yet increasingly difficult, and that to secure it the offerings must be made weekly instead of monthly, and must be made in the form of the money used by the tribe. The sum desired of each was rather large, and it required some sacrifice on the part of each household,—yet, was it not for their beloved Goddess?

"In the course of time there succeeded yet a new minister. He also brought from the Invisible Queen a new message, that on her life depended the security of Croatoan; that her death would be followed by an invasion of the white fiends; yet, to secure that life for another generation, the offerings must be increased in amount, and given daily.

"This last message fell upon the ears of a generation whose oldest member had never personally seen the Queen. They had seen her beautiful face only in the pictures, and had revered her as a goddess; but, now that the demand coming from her was so heavy, they felt that it could only have been made by one so kind as she, in ignorance of their condition. They therefore, through her minister, requested of the Goddess-Queen a personal audience. The minister brought back word from her, that this was impossible. They then sent through him their appeal against an increase of offerings; but he brought back answer that, sad as was their case, their peril from the white fiends, who long before had tried to destroy them and her in the island, was so imminent, that she must insist upon the new taxes named.

"This message caused a terrible excitement, and led to the first division that our tribe had ever known. The older people, in whose minds the traditions which I have related were freshest, were still in alarm about the white fiends, and venerated the living Goddess with growing fear; these were in favour of paying the heavy sum demanded, even at cost of general suffering. The younger of the tribe, in whom the traditions were weaker, resolutely refused to concede the new demands.

When this dispute was nearly at its height a message was brought from the Queén-Goddess demanding that the tax should be raised even by force, if necessary.

"This was the signal of civil war. A terrible struggle ensued; it ended in the younger portion of the tribe leaving the valley, and settling in one adjacent to it. There they set up a government of their own; and while their government resembled in most respects that from which they had seceded, so great was their wrath, that they made it a fundamental law, all swearing solemnly to maintain it, that NO WOMAN SHOULD EVER SIT ON THEIR THRONE. They elected a king and prospered; but their prosperity would have been greater had they not dreaded an attack from the other party to exact the taxes. This apprehension and fear compelled them to withdraw many of their people from work for the defence of their position.

"Meanwhile, the older party, which remained

in occupation in Croatoan, had something else to think of. Deprived of the stalwart arms of many of their best youths, who had gone off to the new government, the burthen imposed on them to preserve the immortality of their tutelary Goddess and Queen became far heavier, and they had less heart to sustain it now that their homes were torn by discord and sorrow. This situation became so grievous that at last the elders of Croatoan resolved that it must end. 'We pay much to be saved,' they said, 'but from what are we saved? What is the use of prolonging our Queen's existence if it means equal prolongation of our misery? Surely, if our tribal traditions be true, she would rather die than destroy her country. As for 'the white fiends,' what could they do worse than these demons of discord, which have torn our once happy Croatoan asunder? Be sure our ever-blessed Queen does not know all this.'

"These counsels led to an overture carried by messengers from Old Croatoan to New Croatoan, asking for a friendly consultation. The result of this was the populations of both valleys proceeded together to the palace, and the king of New Croatoan demanded admission into the presence of the Queen herself.

"This was on the two-hundredth birthday of our Queen. Her minister took the request to the Invisible Queen, and returned with an answer that, although she could not receive his Majesty, she would entertain any proposition he had to submit. So soon as this was uttered, the king ordered his nearest attendants to seize and bind the minister. As they approached, the minister by a touch sounded a huge bell. At that sound some twenty white men in armour appeared at the door. There was a cry ringing through the multitude, 'The white Demons!' others shouted 'Treason!' The women and the men of New Croatoan sprang forward. There was a desperate struggle, the whites sent forth fire from their arms, that same fire of which the tradition remained vivid across two centuries.

Some of the Indian braves fell, wounded by means that they could not understand, but the rest advanced and overpowered the white demons. They found them, when stripped of armour, only men, and liable to die—as they did.

" Tremendous was the revelation of that day ! The palace was entered and no Queen at all found. Instead of an aged woman or goddess, there was found a long table covered with gold and silver plate and many luxuries, with signs of recent carousal. At the head of the table was a ghastly white statue, with the face and form of a woman, its head covered with the wig that I now wear, made of the golden locks, so long admired, of the once living Queen.

" The minister, bound hand and foot, was dragged in, and confessed that the Queen had died over a hundred years before. When she really died, her two ministers, whom in her feebleness she had called to her aid, had concealed her death from the people out of kindness. They dreaded

lest her death might have an evil effect on the
happy tribe, and lest their harmony might be dis-
turbed by intrigues to seize the throne. They
had imposed no burthens on the people, and had
administered affairs according to the dying en-
treaties of their beloved mistress. When they
died, they had passed the secret to their successors,
with earnest admonitions for the welfare of the
tribe. But when others came into power who had
never known the sweet and holy influence of
Virginia's life, they had put forth for their own
selfish ends the false story of her miraculous immortality; and, when they found the people fettered
by this superstition, had made use of their position to extort the offerings and money.

"The extortion of money appears to have
been at first instigated by a party of white men.
They had come to the palace by night and made
their way into it; learning the situation, and that
the people were worshipping at many shrines, as
still alive, a queen long dead, these whites had

prevailed by threats and bribes to make several ministers their tools in extorting money. Every year, at the time of the birthday festival, they came to drink and carouse and bear away the accumulated earnings of the tribe, given to their Invisible Queen; and thus, little by little, the abuse had grown until the poor dead saint had been turned into a ghostly tyrant, destroyer of those she had so devotedly loved and served.

"The white villains and the treacherous minister were now out of the way; the sundered tribe was re-united; Old Croatoan and New Croatoan were names which it was no longer law-ful to utter. But what was to be done? Who was to take the place of the dead Queen? There was no woman to whom that position could be assigned; had there been, a large number of our people had taken a solemn vow never again to serve or support a female ruler. The oath was made in ignorance, but it was one of especial solemnity, such as no Indian has ever been known to break. Yet was there nothing so sweet in the memories of our tribe as the tradition of their golden age, when their blonde Queen reigned. Nor was it forgotten that, even after she had disappeared, the sense of her invisible presence had secured them for a generation the same harmony and happiness. There was a deep longing for a womanly heart, a maternal self-devotion; there was a general horror lest masculine rule should repeat in open forms what it had already accomplished in secret.

"In general council it was settled that the king who had brought this trouble to a crisis, and boldly dragged the conspiracy to light, should be chosen monarch; and that all future kings should be elected by votes of all the tribe—both women and men. But it was further declared that each person so elected should first reign on probation for three years, during which time he should wear a crown of gold. During that period his power should also be very limited; his continu-

ance and full power as monarch must be subject
to ratification by another vote. If he had endeared
himself to the tribe during that time sufficiently
to be confirmed, then he would be entitled to lay
aside the inferior crown of gold, and to receive
upon his head the higher crown made of the
golden locks of the great Queen. He was also
entitled to be no longer addressed as a mere man
or king, but to bear the holiest title known to our
tribe—QUEEN. The ideal of Croatoan is a
woman's heart, and the happy day has but just
come to me when, after three years of devotion to
our tribe, I earned this glory for my head, and the
proud title of Queen !

" You smile," continued the man-queen, " but
perhaps you do not know how hard it is. We
have had king after king who utterly failed to get
beyond that bauble, the crown of gold. They
either demanded taxes and contributions from the
tribe, or put on airs of grandeur, or were impatient
of advice, or rude to the stupid, or had some other

fault which our tribe labels with its one fatal word
—*unqueenly*.   Every one of the kings has tried
his best to obtain this prize, which I am the first
to wear.   Could it only have been gained by
courage, by warlike skill, by strong intellect, or
by learning all that the tribe knows, by sentiment-
ality or by effeminacy, this aureole would not now
for the first time have been brought out from its
hiding-place.   I say hiding-place, for since one of
the kings tried to seize the crown by violence, it
has been placed in the hands of the women of our
tribe for concealment until one should be voted
worthy to wear it.   One king tried to gain it by
holding the tribe in awe of his majesty, and the
men all voted against him ; another aimed at the
same end with frequent tears and occasional
hysterics, and the women all voted against him.

"How did I gain it ?   It is almost a mystery
to myself.   As a boy I was very active ; my chief
ambition was to outrun and outleap other boys, to
stand on my head longest, or to walk on my hands.

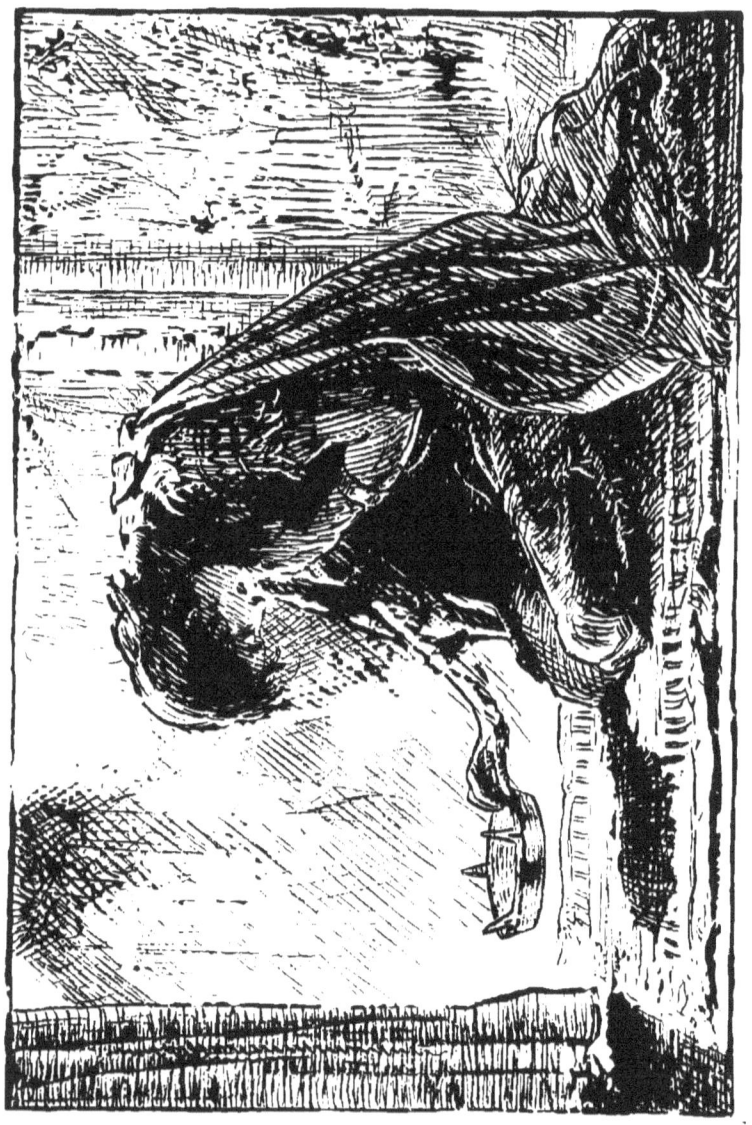

" Contend now with thyself."

My mother told me, as every mother in Croatoan
tells her children, the legend of our tribe, and
every week, on the day when its curtain is regularly withdrawn, I came to gaze on the picture of
our first Queen. Once, when the first shade of
twilight was falling, and others had gone away,
I remained alone in this room gazing up to the
blue eyes ; when lo, they appeared to beam with
life, the lips parted, and a gentle voice came to
my ear—' Thou hast succeeded in contending with
others; contend now with thyself!' As these
words were uttered, a hand shook me ; it was that
of the doorkeeper, who said, ' This is not the place
to sleep ; you came near being locked up here for
the night !' It had been a dream; but it remained
with me.

"How to contend with myself! As years
came on it became plain enough what self it was
with which I had to contend ; but, alas ! this self
outleaped and outran me. On one occasion I
succeeded. Our tribe had annual games on the

great Queen's birthday, and once had offered a fine
prize to the youth who should first reach a certain
goal.   In that race I ran.   My swiftest competitor
was a youth whom I had previously surpassed in
various contests.   This time, however, he kept
abreast of me for some distance, and the chances
were even on his side ; but suddenly, when we
were distant from the crowd, a dog ran across his
path and barked before him ; this threw him back,
and I won the race.   No one saw his disaster but
myself ; the defeated youth said nothing about the
dog.   The judges came with dancing maidens to
give me the prize.   But over their heads I saw
the beaming blue eyes, the moving lips which bade
me contend with myself ; so, by our Queen's grace,
I was enabled to decline the prize, and, having told
the incident of the dog, claimed for my antagonist
another race.   In this I did my best, but was
defeated.

" This piece of self-denial was not done by my
own strength, nor did I credit myself with it ; it

was the inspiration of our Queen ; but it had so sweet a taste that it taught me the value of invisible prizes. When I had reached the age of twenty a new king had to be chosen, and the ballots were found to be in my favour. I was astounded. When the first glow of pride was over, my golden crown seemed turned to dross. I sat on the throne only to find it hard as flint. How dared I sit in the place of the queenly One who had created a happy tribe, and whose transmitted memory made its conscience ? After the first year the hope of wearing the halo of that saint rose in my mind, and I ardently aspired to it. At the end of the second year it seemed that my chances were good when the people all gathered to applaud my efforts. But, only a month before my third year was completed, an event occurred which raised between me and the coveted prize a terrible barrier.

"It had for some time appeared evident to the wisest of our tribe—as I considered them—

that the preservation in our homes of the Queen's shrines had an evil effect on them, especially upon the children. These shrines had been erected under the belief that she was still living miraculously, whereas it was now known that she was no supernatural being, but had died when her time came, like others. Yet it was found that around these shrines the superstition which originated them still lingered, even grew, and in that atmosphere other superstitions flourished. Under the belief that she was a goddess the household pictures of the Queen had received additions, and around her head had been painted circles of light. In this nimbus her simple human virtues were dimmed. Parents found it difficult to make the child, which had no miraculous rays round its head, look up to the glorified Queen as an example of what each might become. It was also the custom from of old to lay before these shrines, as offerings, comforts and luxuries which none thereafter would touch, whereas they were often required by the aged and the invalid. The children, and even some of the older people, had a sort of belief that these offerings were required by the Queen, or at least pleased her, and that in return for them she sometimes granted favours. From this it was an easy step of faith to believe that the more precious the offerings the greater would be the favours. All this showed such a tendency to increase, that our sages remarked with pain the growth of a generation which hoped to gain virtue by other means than being virtuous, to acquire benefits by favouritism, instead of by fulfilling the natural conditions of labour and prudence by which such benefits could be reached alike by all, whether able to afford offerings to the shrines or not. They also judged that, by these superstitions concerning the ancient Queen, the real spirit of her life and nature of her service were being sacrificed and lost sight of. They therefore brought forward a proposition that these household shrines should be discouraged by a pro-

clamation from the throne, and that the king should
set an example by removing the shrine which had
long stood in the palace.

"With these arguments I sympathised, but
found that a decided majority were against us.
This majority had entire faith that I would protect their shrines and usages, which had become
symbols of their religion, and that I could never
be prevailed upon to commit the sacrilege of removing the palace-shrine of the great and good
Queen. They even freely hinted of 'white
demons' again, which would punish such sacrilege ;
so that old superstition had not quite perished.
The more the people talked in this way, the more
was I convinced that the sages of our tribe were
justified in their fears as to the moral effect of the
household shrines. But these sages were few,
and their voices were drowned in the clamorous
hostility of the many to the proposed reform. It
even became evident that the step to which the
few called me would prove revolutionary. So sure

was the majority that a devoted lover of our Queen, like myself, would never take the side of her 'enemies'—as the reformers were freely called —that they unanimously agreed to leave it to me whether their shrines should stand or fall.

"This position of arbiter was sprung upon me before I had been able to lay before the tribe my views. It was evident too that they were moved by sentiment, and that the reasonings which had convinced me would be lost on most of them. I was suddenly called upon to act, and, alas! to act rightly was to cut myself off from all possibility of wearing the queenly crown which had seemed to come within a few months' reach of me. Those who sympathised with my convictions about the shrines were obliged to tell me that the act they proposed would certainly destroy my hopes of promotion to the honour which had roused all my ambition, and that my crown would pass to the head of the most noisy and superstitious defender of the popular faith. Perhaps the hardest trial before me was this, that I would no longer be custodian of our Queen's portrait, which for a long time it had been my daily delight to gaze upon.

"A certain day—the Queen's birthday—had been appointed for the tribe to assemble and receive my decision. I was in terrible affliction. Never shall I forget the eve of that day. On the spot where I had crouched as a boy, and gazed upon the beautiful face till I slept, and heard her speak in my dream, I now passed the night with tears. As I sat before the picture, longing to know what I should do, the weary hours sounded out amid the darkness—one, two, three: they seemed to come almost in continuous peal, so hurriedly did the day approach which I would fain have deferred for ever. Beside me burned a single lamp. I suppose I fell asleep. There passed before me the days of childhood; then of boyhood; I seemed to live over again every day and hour of my existence, till that twilight evening arrived when the doorkeeper had awakened me in the palace.

"Then, lo! once more the blue eyes beamed—once more the lips of the picture moved; what would they say? This time I felt they would solve my present doubts, and plead either for or against the shrines! What they said was this: ' Thou hast succeeded in contending with others; contend now with thyself!'

"I was awakened by voices at the palace-door. Starting up, I looked upon the picture. There it was in smiling beauty, as it came from a mother's hand. A true woman! What fortitude was seated on that brow, what love and truth suffused that face, which traitors had sought to turn to a shelter of selfishness and falsehood! Already I was a king; now would I be a Queen; ay, even though an invisible Queen, whose golden locks and great title should be worn by others!

" My mind was made up. The doors of the palace were flung wide; the people pressed in

with loud applause, and stood in ranks before me.
I told them my decision, and gave them the reasons
which had convinced me that their cherished
shrines represented a delusion and were bringing
on a danger. As I proceeded, there were cries of
dismay, which swelled to shouts of anger. 'Tear
the crown from his head!' I answered by removing it and laying it beside me. 'Protect the
shrine!' was the next cry. A number of the
leaders rushed into the room which had long been
the oratory of the palace; but they found there
no shrine. In the early dawn I had removed it.
The populace were now almost frantic. Though
the reformers pleaded with them that they had
agreed to abide by my decision, they were not
listened to; I was dragged away through the
roads, amid the taunts of a clamorous mob, and
they placed on my head a paper crown, labelled,
'Our good Queen's Enemy.' At length I was
taken to a dark room, in which the ever-notorious
traitor, the last minister who had oppressed the

tribe, had been shut up previous to his execution. That a like fate awaited me I did not doubt.

In my dark prison I remained long. The first day brought me no sign from the outer world,— not even any food. Towards the close of the second day a little Indian corn was thrown in at the door by an unseen hand. I ate it hungrily, and lay down on the floor; I never before had a sleep so sweet. Many weary hours succeeded; I supposed it had been determined to leave me to starve. At length another handful of corn was thrown to me. My brain now began to be filled with fearful fancies. In my increasingly feverish dreams I saw the men and women whose counsels I had taken undergoing execution. Now and then distant shouts reached me; I knew the excitement was still raging: it was an agony which made me forget hunger and thirst, that I could not know how it fared with those brave reformers who had withstood the popular superstition, and what was the fate of our cause.

"After a longer interval than usual, a loaf of bread was put in at my door, with a cup of water. What luxury! All the delicacies of my life in a palace were poor beside that bread and water, sweetened by the first recovery of hope. Day after day this bread and water came through weeks that seemed years, but no human voice did I hear. Did I say none? There was one; once in a dream, a gentle voice said once more, 'Thou hast succeeded in contending with others; contend now with thyself.' But the voice was sad, and the face which rose before me was very sad; the blue eyes were filled with tears. This vision impressed my weakened nerves as an omen, and its melancholy meaning was confirmed by the fact that for more than a day and night the bread and water were withheld.

"At length, faint with hunger and apprehension, I heard a step at my door. My heart whispered, It is the approach of Death. It was not so. The door opened, and my mother entered. I rushed to embrace her, but she spoke not. She placed beside me the best food she could afford, then quickly, with a look of tender compassion, left me. In the doorway behind her I caught the face of our chief antagonist, and her parting look told me she was admitted only under pledge of silence. But a mother's look needs no words. I saw that the moment was critical, but there was no reason for despair.

"The better food came regularly, but it was no longer brought by my mother; it was silently placed beside me by the hands of the chief 'defender of the faith,' as he had been styled. And, although he spoke no word, it amazed me much to observe that his face bore no sign of hostility. Indeed, as day succeeded day, his face appeared rather friendly than otherwise. This, however, gave me disquiet, for I saw in it evidence that he and the party of superstition had won the day, and in their strength could afford to be lenient to the defeated. I knew that the time

E

for the election of a new king must now be very
near; and once, when the shrine-defender entered
with my food, his face was so radiant that I felt
certain he was to succeed me on the throne.
This filled me with gloomy forebodings, for in
solitude I had reviewed the entire question, and
was more than ever convinced that the future
happiness and progress of our tribe depended on
the success of our cause.

"At last there came a day when the 'defender'
appeared at the open door without food. He
bade me come forth. I hastened into the sunshine, and there found the tribe gathered. I was
in a maze, not knowing what fate awaited me.
Then strong arms seized me; I was set upon a
throne; the crown of gold was placed upon my
head; preceded by bands of singers and dancers,
my throne was borne on the shoulders of young
men to the palace. Arriving there, I was seated
beneath that picture. I learned then that daily
since my imprisonment the debate had gone on;

one by one most of our opponents had been convinced of the justice of our cause; and all had .
been convinced that our good Queen would have
more honoured my costly fidelity to convictions
than any servile and selfish compliance. So had
our Saint passed from fictitious to true immortality,
and reached forth her hand to save her tribe.
When the vote was taken—and by a compromise it
had been agreed that I should have no communi-
cation with the tribe until it was taken—every
ballot was cast in favour of the prisoner. It
might not have been so, but that the chief
defender of the shrines arose and said he had
learned that it was the true halo of a woman that
she could lay down her life for others, and he felt
that he must be a very unwomanly man who could
wear a crown which one had laid aside for a
prison out of love to their tribe.

"You may think others should tell you this
story rather than myself; but I think I can re-
hearse it without pride, or perhaps with only a little

pride ; for when, amid acclamations, this wig was placed on my head, and the proud title of Queen was awarded me, I never felt more lowly than in that glorious hour. I knew that it was with my lower unqueenly self that a contest had been waged and won ; but I realised that when my own hair and face were artificially changed to suggest resemblance to the picture there, it was but a faint approach to the truth that my sacrifice and victory were those of one who would have been a poor savage but for the influence of a humanised ideal —an Invisible Queen."

When the King had ended this story, the Europeans went to move about the valley, and converse with the inhabitants. In their homes they found portraits of the first Queen, but no halo around her head save the glory of her hair, and no shrines. They heard from all lips praises of Queen II., then reigning, and how manly she was, or, as some said, how womanly he was. They saw on every side evidences that in a region where

Spaniards, Italians, Frenchmen, Englishmen, had
sought a realm of gold, had massacred thousands
in their search for it, yet found it not, the first pure
child and true woman cast helpless into the arms
of savages had been able to create a realm that
gold was inadequate to symbolise. They wandered
about as if under a charm from day to day, and
two weeks passed before one ventured to remind
another of their yacht awaiting them on the coast.
Then some said, " Let it stay there till it sinks!"
another said, " Why should we ever return?" a
third said, " If our families believe we have gone
to Paradise, will they be wrong?" But when
another week had passed, these men found that in
each of them there was an invisible queen. To be
manly involved also being womanly, and in the far
world were hearts waiting and watching for their
return.

It was with tears that they left Croatoan. It
was also with vows that they would return again,
bringing their loved ones with them. Leaving to

the kindly natives all the books they had brought, they departed carrying promises of welcome should they return. Their eyes were bandaged, and they were led away for a few miles, and left with ample food for their journey to the coast. Ere long they were sailing for the White Island of the north.

What welcome in dear English homes! What receptions in political circles and learned societies! "They were just in time." The House of Lords and splendid marriages await the noblemen; of the others one is wanted to enter Parliament for his family borough; another must be Fellow of the Royal Society; a third fill the vacant chair at Oxford, and the artists are already Academicians.

How joyful all this to the seven—had they never seen Croatoan! Now each meets the new step in his career with a vague consciousness that it is meant for somebody else no longer living. They amaze their families and friends by strange reluctances and hesitations; and at length are compelled to confess that their hearts are roaming

away to the far-off island.   At this friends smile,
relatives wonder ; but gradually society and life
weave their subtle threads around the voyagers ;
Croatoan remains as a pleasant tale, to which many
a child listens while seated on the knees of grave
gentlemen.

For the passing years bring them homes and
families of their own, full occupation, fame.   They
have little time to dwell with early memories ; but
now and then, when affairs have not gone quite
smoothly, each is as likely as not to say, " I sometimes wish I was living in Croatoan."   And rarely
does each half-sigh, if heard, fail to arouse a chorus
of little voices calling again for the oft-told tale.

Gradually our seven voyagers of early days
outgrew their dream of returning to visit the
gentle islanders ; but, on the other hand, that
which had become a family-legend in each household had steadily taken root in the hearts of their
wives and children.   These dreamed and dreamed
of a tour to the land of the good man-queen.

And in that circuitous way by which even pale-faced ladies sometimes reach their ends, a voyage to Croatoan was actually decided on. One evening, through some conspiracy, the seven voyagers of "The Fancy" found themselves around a dinner-table with their wives; and next morning each was surprised to hear from his spouse, and his children were certain she was right, that he had pledged himself, with a libation of old port, to sail with the rest for Croatoan, during the near summer.

*   *   *   *   **

On a bright morning in June, the little coast-steamer, "The Iron City," started out from Baltimore with an English party which had chartered it. These were our seven, with their wives and children. They took a strong little boat for an indefinite time, and a pilot warranted to know all things knowable about southern islands. After a considerable voyage they saw an island on the Virginian coast, and the pilot said it was Croatoan. This elicited shouts of joy from the merry company, and they steamed straight to it. Having landed, and walked some little distance, they met a ragged white man driving a two-wheeled cart, and he told them they were not in Croatoan ; he believed it was farther down.

A little later " The Iron City " was making its way southward, and after hours that seemed ages, another island appeared. On this too they landed, but after exploring it until late in the evening, they encountered another white man, who told them they were not in Croatoan. But this was not all; he told them he had never heard of Croatoan, and that there had been no Indians in any of those islands for a hundred years.

Our Europeans were more silent than usual, as they repaired to their steamer ; that night they slept somewhat uneasily in their berths. Next morning they questioned their pilot more closely about his knowledge of the coast, and several noted that his answers about Croatoan were vague and evasive. Still they steamed southward, for island after island beckoned them onward. But, alas! while some of these, where they landed, were found uninhabited, the sparse whites of others had never heard of the one they sought, nor ever seen any Indians.

With a growing pain in every heart, they steamed in and out at inlets, hovered about promontories, explored islands and all shores that even faintly suggested the old landing-place. All in vain! After weeks of fruitless search, they turned from the Florida coast, and reluctantly turned the prow of "The Iron City" northward again.

They had travelled in this direction for some days when a severe storm sprang up, and it was found necessary to put in towards the shore. The steamer found an opening in a bar of sand, and good shelter behind it. But now, when the storm had passed, one of the artists thought the place presented some familiar features. After a little quiet consultation, and without raising in their wives and children expectations that might be disappointed, the seven middle-aged gentlemen resolved to go on a little excursion ashore. Great was their delight when they found point after point which vaguely recalled the visit of years before. They were still uncertain ; but one of them remembered that when they had left he had chipped on a rock, at the spot where the bandages were removed, the word CROATOAN. Full of eagerness they walked forward, and finally, sure enough, they came to the rock on which the word was still clearly visible.

But where were the merry maidens ? Where were the gentle captors with the curious eye-bandages ? They saw none. They shouted and sang, and tried to awaken attention, but they saw no human being, nor trace of the past save the word carved on rock. It is not pleasing to linger with the story of their disappointment. For two days they wandered in that lonely region, sleeping on leaves at night ; but it was all as a land which

never before was trodden by human footsteps.
To their calls in every valley, only cold echoes
answered. They saw merry grey squirrels leaping
from bough to bough ; were startled by the
upward flutter of quails ; bright gemmed serpents
looked at them and glided away ; the Virginian
nightingale lit up each wood with its torchlike
wings ; and the song of the mocking-bird blended
with the mournful note of the turtle-dove, which
seemed, like themselves, to be seeking some lost joy.

They never found Croatoan again. As they
sorrowfully sought the sea again the seven were
silent. A profound unutterable regret filled them.
One said at last, " It seems that it is only with
bandaged eyes one can ever see Croatoan." And
when at length they were about going on board
"The Iron City" which lay black on the blue water,
an artist said, " Perhaps we should have had
better luck had we been twenty years younger, and
drifted here before the wind on our old yacht."

" By the way," remarked one when they were

all on board, "The Fancy was a beautiful yacht, what has become of it?" "It rotted in London Docks long ago," was the reply.

One little boy, who caught this question and answer, said, "Papa, why did you let pretty 'Fancy' rot?" The father made no reply; he pointed the child to a flight of sea-birds. But presently the boy turned and said, as tears of bitter disappointment filled his eyes—"Mother, when I get back, I will build another yacht, and call it 'The Fancy,' and sail across the ocean. Will I not then find the Queen of Croatoan?"

THE FANCY.

BERNARD AND ROBIN REDBREAST

BERNARD & ROBIN REDBREAST.

A LITTLE orphan named Bernard, who loved to
wander in a wood near the house of his uncle,
with whom he lived, went out one summer morning, and returning late to breakfast, told a mar-
vellous story. An angel, he said, had come down
to him through the bright morning air, had borne
him in her arms up to rosy clouds, where she sang
a sweet song. Unfortunately this boy's uncle
and guardian was prosaic, and the angels he believed in were prosaic as himself, and he pro-
nounced the boy's narrative "a lie." The same
might, with equal truth, be said of Shakspere's
Tempest; but, however much the prosaic world
may like the charm of romance, it rarely sees any
fledgling touched with the lustre of imagination
but to try and make it commonplace as the rest.

F

Thus our little Bernard, who told his adventure with the angel, was flogged for telling "a lie." Knowing very well that it was no lie at all, he was indignant, and concluded to leave his home.

After he had wandered a few hours, Bernard was very weary, and it began to snow hard, which made him cold. The wind and sky seemed to be taking sides with his uncle, and he almost thought he must have been wrong after all, since now, in his sore need, no angel descended to fold him in her arms. Could that other angel, that shone so bright but cost him so dear, have been merely a dream? Perhaps he might have gone back home had he not felt uncertain about the way, which was hidden by snow. The earth and sky were as inhospitable as his uncle's house, and seemed to be flogging him over again.

Our little wanderer was very cold indeed; but presently he reached a fir-tree, which offered him some slight shelter, and a bed of its soft needles to lie upon. He wondered, if he lay there

"A merry voice cried to him, 'Cheer up !'"

and died, whether the robins would come and cover him with leaves; and he was much pained to observe that there were no leaves around which might make him a shroud.

While these tragical thoughts were passing through the troubled mind of the Boy, who was blowing on his fingers to keep them warm, and just as he was preparing to creep in under the fir-tree, a merry voice cried to him, "Cheer up!" Looking round to the spot from which it proceeded, he perceived a Robin; he almost smiled, unhappy as he was, at his notion that the bird had spoken to him. But the Robin again, and more clearly than before, said, "Cheer up!"

"I don't see much to cheer up at," said Bernard.

"We don't expect a Boy to see much," replied the bird.

"Who is 'we'?" asked the Boy, too cold to be particular about grammar.

"We birds."

"Can't a Boy see as much as a bird?"

"Oh dear, no,"—and here the Robin broke into an immoderate fit of laughter.

"Can't a man?" asked the Boy, modestly.

"Why, how can he?" returned the bird. "Has he wings? How many men are out playing in this snow-storm? They're all shut up or muffled up. Man's a muff." And the Robin laughed again, rather scornfully.

"I thought a B-bo—that is, a man, was a great deal better than a bird," said the Boy. "Even I am bigger than you."

"That's just the difficulty," said the bird. "Just now I saw a poor horse shivering over there—you needn't get on tiptoes, *you* can't see him—who is bigger than you. Trouble is, there's too much of you. If you were small enough, now, you could hide under a leaf, creep into a hole, do a hundred things that would make you comfortable. But if you were a bird, you'd have warm feathers and warm exercise, and that's equal to carrying one's house and fireside about with one."

" I'd have to eat," suggested Bernard.

" Yes, but now you're so big that there's too much to be fed. Why, you're a walking larder. You'll have to spend all your life just to live. I've just picked a berry, and it made me a good dinner. Where are you going to dine ?"

" I'm sure I don't know," said the Boy piteously, " unless I can get back home."

" And be whipped again every time you have a bright fancy, or see an angel ! and be made to learn hard lessons all day, which, after all, leave you such an ignoramus, that you don't even know that a bird is a better and nobler being than a man !"

" What's ignoramus ?" inquired the Boy.

" Ignoramus !" said the bird ; " why, it's a person who wouldn't know the difference between this fir and a pine—doesn't know anything."

" How do you know so much about boys ?" inquired Bernard.

" I was a boy myself once," answered the

Robin, "and oh, what a sad time I had of it! But I ran away and became a Robin!"

"How did you manage it? Can I become a Robin? I should like it." And here the Boy blew on his fingers again.

"How did I manage it? I was evolved."

"Ewhiched?" asked the Boy, getting rather confused.

"Evolved. It's too long a story to tell the whole, but I threw away everything about me which I found useless, heavy, and uncomfortable. When I was a boy, there were so many large spaces about me that people thought they were made to be smacked: I saw that birds' cheeks and other parts were too small to be smacked. Then, while I was a boy, I found I had to learn a great many words, and it took long sentences to make myself understood, and if I didn't get every word right I was scolded; but I listened to the birds, and became certain that they could tell a great deal in one or two pretty sounds. People don't need many words when the tone tells what they mean. My hands, when I was a boy, troubled me most of all, I believe. They were always getting dirty, and I had to wash them ; they got cold ; they got cut ; and people were always making me work, and asking me what my hands were made for. Now, I saw that the birds had got rid of *their* hands. They had made them into wings by which they could get out of the way when any one would disturb them."

" Not always," said the boy, "people sometimes shoot them, or put them in cages."

" Alas, yes !" said the Robin, "even when Evolution has carried us up to the ornithomorphic phase, survivals are found in our environment which are discordant with ideal existence." And here the Robin dashed a tear from its eye, and picked a worm from a leaf beside it.

The Boy did not see this last performance, and if he had, he could hardly have challenged the Robin's consistency, since he was compelled to answer, " What is 'existence'? and what is 'survivals' and 'envirulmint'? and what is 'ornipho-thormeck'? I don't understand you at all."

" Pardon me," said the bird, " I forgot I was talking to a boy. I was levelling my remarks down to the mind of a man. Well, what I was going to say is this : I found that the birds were things that had thrown off a great mass of useless flesh, and bones, and talk, and wants ; that their wings enabled them to get out of reach of most enemies ; and then I found that the smaller birds were happiest because there was less of them to tempt ogres, whether with wings or guns, less weight to carry about, and they could fly faster than the cannibal-birds, in which dwell the souls of wicked men ; and next I found that of all birds the Robin was happiest, because men, and even boys, have a notion that they ought not to kill or cage Robins. So I chose to be evolved into a Robin— and oh, what a load of troubles I got rid of ! I am now a happy little world floating about. I see splendid sights, have a dear little nest, am never too cold nor too hot, nor——"

" But *how* did you get to be a bird, when you were a boy ?" inquired Bernard, unable to restrain his curiosity and impatience.

" Oh, I forgot that point," answered the Robin. " But now that you ask me, I don't think you can understand my explanation. Not one man even in ten thousand could understand it, perhaps not one in ten thousand five hundred. I didn't exactly understand it myself till I became a Robin, for I found it could only be told in bird-language."

" I want to hear it, any way," said the Boy.

" Well, then," said the Robin, "in the first place I prothelicised myself,— peliously not buliously,— and having thus become arimanthous, it was easy to find the faliad fasiant. The rest may be easily imagined."

" Oh dear," said Bernard ; " I believe I can't be a bird, and I am hungry, but not so cold as I was."

"That comes of looking at my red breast," said the Robin. "What you'd better do is to go home, take your flogging bravely, think over what I've said to you, and do your best, and some day, when you get your wings, we may meet again—cheer up!" And off flew the Robin merrily. Bernard looked after the Robin, felt sorry it had gone, and called it back again. While talking with it he had forgotten that he was cold and hungry, but now his wants came back upon him. Yet somehow he did not feel so miserable as before; he felt his courage rising, and also his common sense. He resolved that he would take the Robin's advice; he would go home, and he would be brave and quiet under any punishment that might await him. It was a long way and a hard way back, but the Boy found first one and then another familiar landmark, and succeeded in reaching home. He found the family in great distress at his absence; they had been searching for him, and finding it vain, had

come back at nightfall. They were in dread lest
their further search next morning would find him
frozen in the snow.

And now did Bernard find out how much love
his uncle and aunt had for him, even though they
were severe, and could not get it out of their heads
that his pretty fancies were falsehoods. Perhaps
they had just found it out too. When he came in
all covered with snow, his aunt clasped him in her
arms and covered him with kisses. The uncle
was startled because the Boy came and stood
before him and said, "You can whip me now; I
am not afraid to be whipped. After a while I
shall get my wings."

"My dear boy," said the uncle, " I do not
wish to whip you ; I will never strike you again
—there."

It was a wise resolution to come to, and perhaps this uncle and aunt would have come to it
sooner if they had only been able to take example
by the way of Robins with their nestlings.

Bernard did not tell the story of his talk with the Robin to anybody at that time; indeed, when he had eaten a comfortable supper, slept warmly and without a dream, and lay thinking it all over next morning—for his aunt wouldn't let him get up at the usual time—he smiled at himself for ever thinking that he had really heard a Robin talk. Still he found every word it had seemed to say ringing in his ears and through his thoughts.

After that curious adventure Bernard changed a good deal in his ways and manners. Not that he was an ill-natured boy before; on the contrary, he had always been good-natured; but now he became more affectionate, less noisy, and not so much in the way as he used to be. It looked as if he remembered the Robin's happiness in not being big, and was trying to fill less space than formerly. His aunt said now she believed that boy "would live on a few crumbs, quite content," if she'd let him.

Bernard also talked less than before his experience in the snowstorm, and what he left off in words he made up in the sweet tones with which he spoke them. If he had to say " no " to anybody, he said it so gently that it was as much as to say " I am truly sorry that I am not able to do what you wish, but you may feel sure that I will help you whenever I can." All that Bernard said in his look and voice, so that it was pleasanter to hear his " no " than many people's " yes."

Bernard was very fond of singing. And when he got larger and went to a large school, the other boys would sometimes stop their sports to hear Bernard sing a ballad. There was such a glow about his heart, he was so genial and cheery, that even the school-bully said he'd "as lief strike a robin as Bernard."

At the same time that Bernard was kind and gentle, he was very courageous ; he was never afraid of wind, hail, or snow ; he was able to jump, swim, skate, and play cricket with the rest. But he also learnt so well, and was so quick in understanding, that the master said that Bernard was "like some winged creature among four-footed kinds." He told this to Bernard's uncle; if the boy had heard it, he would have remembered his Robin of the fir-tree.

But perhaps this was the most curious and pleasant thing of all. We cannot forget that little Bernard was whipped and ran away because he told a story about an angel carrying him up into the rosy dawn, which his good but humdrum uncle thought was merely a lie. But when Bernard now came back from school in vacations, his uncle was never tired of listening to his ballads. These ballads were composed by Bernard himself, though it was a long time before any one knew that, and they told just as strange tales as that about the angel which once brought him a flogging; but he now found that when he made his stories into rhyme, and especially when he sang them, he might tell as many big stories as he liked, and his uncle was delighted with them. Bernard wrote

and sang about birds that made little rhymes,
fairies that nestled in babies' dimples, giants whose
hearts were blocks of ice, but could be melted by a
tiny fay, called Sunbeam; and one of his ballads—
the one his uncle liked best—was about a restless
Raindrop who slid down to the earth on a rainbow
and was married to a little flower, to whom he
gave a bit of the rainbow he had brought down
with him—on which account she was ever after
called Violet, all her descendants bearing the same
name, and wearing the dress which the Eve-Violet
got from the rainbow. Bernard's uncle did, indeed, wish to know how it was that dress held out
so long, and was big enough to supply so many
flowers, but his nephew met that difficulty by
adding a verse which told how the first Mother
Violet, being a wise and industrious wife, worked
until she found a way of making other dresses
after the pattern of her own, and taught this
secret to her daughters, who taught it to theirs, so
that the weaving of such dresses became an heir-

G

loom in the family. Bernard's uncle declared that this was real poetry, and never knew that it was the same thing he had once tried to flog out of his little nephew. Still it must be said for him that Bernard had not then learned his finer art from the Robin.

Bernard grew, indeed, to be a great poet; and those who talked and wrote about him wondered how much he always found in very little things. Some one wrote about him—" This strange poet seems somehow to have learned the language of birds : he finds as much in a robin as other poets fancy in an angel."

THE NATURALIST, THE CHILD,

AND

THE HUMMING-BIRD

THE NATURALIST, THE CHILD, AND THE HUMMING-BIRD.

A NATURALIST, passionately devoted to his scientific pursuits, had a little daughter who often looked with wonder upon the curious things that lay about her father's house. The strange stuffed animals, the fossils, and other objects which made up his collection, had a fascination for this child, whose name was Mildred; but she had tried in vain to make out their meaning. She had once or twice asked her father—now, alas! her only parent —to explain them to her. He was an affectionate father, provided for his child's little wants, loved to play with her; but either because he did not think science suitable for the mind of Mildred's sex, or because he thought his daughter too young for such studies—perhaps for both reasons—he had put her off on those occasions; once, indeed, so sharply—dearly as he loved her, but being very busy at the time—that she never asked such questions again. Mildred's unsatisfied and growing curiosity, left thus to find its own answers, found strange and unhappy ones. The big saurian figures took on a kind of life, and surrounded her pillow with fantastic shapes; the stuffed animals prowled, the huge birds with beaks like swords flitted about her little chamber; skulls grinned, claws clutched at her; and when the child was supposed to be fast asleep, she was really passing hours of excitement and dread amid these queer creatures, to which her fancy had given life. She dared not tell her sufferings to any one, but they told on her : her father saw with anxiety and alarm his once bright and lovely Mildred had lost her childhood, and become a pining girl, drooping in health and spirits, despite his care for her. At last she became a confirmed invalid ; yet none of

"The big saurian figures took on a kind of life, and surrounded her pillow with fantastic shapes."

the physicians around could tell what was the matter with her.

One day the naturalist was walking in his garden with his darling invalid, and they stopped for some time in the warm sunshine to admire a humming-bird, which, like a winged gem, flashed from bower to bower, dipping its long beak down into the long horns of the honeysuckles so nicely fitted to it. He had long wished to examine more closely this beautiful little bird and to observe its habits ; so the naturalist and his daughter made efforts to catch it alive, and Mildred, with a skilful toss of her veil, succeeded.

The little beauty was carried into the house triumphantly. But, alas ! very soon after it was taken captive, the pretty thing began to droop. Its feathers lost much of their lustre, its eye became dim, and it seemed about to die. The naturalist brought in fresh clusters of honeysuckle, honey was smeared on its beak, sugared water was held to it, every device his skill could invent was tried ;

in vain—the humming-bird drooped more and more, and lay with filmed eyes on its side. At last it was determined that the little thing should be set free again.

It was gently placed out on the grass, and the father and daughter stood apart motionless, watching closely. The fresh air and grass revived the bird a little, and it hopped feebly along for a few feet, then lay still as if dead; presently it went a little farther,—a yard or two,—the naturalist and his daughter softly following. Then they saw the humming-bird devour a tiny green spider; when lo, as by magic, its lustres all came back; its eye brightened, and it darted up again among the honeysuckles, flashing here and there, as if made up of rubies and emeralds!

Then the naturalist and his daughter collected a large number of these little green spiders, and he said, "To-morrow we will try to catch another humming-bird."

But while the father was yet asleep, in the

early morning, Mildred rose up and was soon gliding from bower to bower, flinging her veil here and there, trying to catch one of the humming-birds. She was so absorbed in these efforts, that the breakfast - bell rang for her in vain; the servant came from her room to report that " Miss Mildred was not there," and the father was just recovering from the shock of such an unheard-of event, when in sprang his girl with a humming-bird safely swinging in her veil.

This indeed was a joy. The humming-bird was placed in a very large cage, which Mildred decorated constantly with fresh honeysuckle and other flowers, while the naturalist kept one corner well stored with green spiders. Every day, while her father was engaged upon other scientific work, Mildred watched the movements and habits of this little creature, and made careful note of them on paper; and every evening she read this day's report to the naturalist. As she read, he now and then mentioned that it behaved like this or that other bird, of which he told her something ; and in this way he fell into the habit of talking to her about many things in nature. After a time, by the help of Mildred's reports, the naturalist wrote an account of the manners and customs of humming-birds, and if any reader of this book knows anything much about that most exquisite of all birds, it came from that essay, and chiefly from Mildred's observations. And I may add that after Mildred had made her observations, and all she and her father could learn about the humming-bird was put in print, they resolved to let the little bird go free. So one day they opened the cage, and it darted out ; but the window was left open. After a time the breezy whirr of its wings, seen only as a tinted halo when it flies, was heard, and it returned to its flowery cage. Thenceforth it came and went as it pleased ; the cage had become a home.

But what of the invalid ? She had disappeared,

and in her place the naturalist saw once more his darling Mildred, with healthy colour and sparkling eye.

"How is it, my daughter," he said one day, "that you have managed without any doctors, better than with them? You have become so much stronger and livelier and happier that I hardly know you. You must introduce me to yourself."

"Shall I tell you my little secret, father?" said the girl, smiling. "Well, do you know that ever since we caught that first humming-bird together, and set it out on the grass, and saw how it came to life again,—ever since then I have felt as if I too had eaten some kind of green spider."

"You!" said the naturalist, but not too seriously, for he knew Mildred sometimes talked in fun. "Why, the last thing I should say was good for a girl is a green spider!"

"Or for a little bird either," said Mildred.

"But somehow that darling humming-bird began my knowing about the other things,—the big bones, preserved lizards, stuffed birds, snakes. Why, I'm not afraid of one of them now! They're my friends now!"

Mildred said no more, but kissed her father and went off to her pillow, to dream of nothing worse than flitting amid myrtle and honeysuckle in the form of a humming-bird. But her father did not go to sleep quite so quickly; he lay thinking a long time, and next day—and for many a happy day afterwards—his daughter heard from him all he could tell of every form in his collection. Mildred's young mind, fed on facts, was no longer fed upon by ugly fancies or fictions. The naturalist had learned that a man may know a good deal about bones, stones, animals, plants, and minerals, and yet find out finer secrets than they can tell him by sometimes paying close and loving attention to little birds and little girls, and finding out on what little things (a tiny green spider, say, or a question answered) the springs of life and death may depend.

THE BUCKET AND THE ACORN

H

THE BUCKET AND THE ACORN.

An oaken Bucket for many years had been in the habit of going to a venerable pump, and gradually learned to regard that pump as sacred, and the chief end of all created things to hold its holy water as it might be pumped into them. This ancient Bucket was one day left standing under the venerable pump long enough to look around it. Its attention was attracted by an Acorn, to which some of the pump-water streamed, but which did not seem to have any mouth with which to receive it. Presently a maid came for the Bucket, and in bearing it away, trod on this Acorn, which seemed to be the end of it.

At a later period the Bucket observed a tiny

shoot of green growing out of the spot where the Acorn had been trodden. From time to time, whenever it came to be filled at the pump, the Bucket observed this growth, and it was somewhat scandalised by the fact that though water was continually streaming to it from the holy pump, it did not hold any of it at all : not a twig or leaf of it shaped itself to a Bucket, or even a can or a mug ; but all appeared to spread themselves into the air aimlessly and to expand recklessly.

The Bucket repeatedly exhorted what it considered and called a naughty Acorn on its duty to receive and hold the sacred stream ; but the latter was fast mounting up to be a sapling, and paid little attention to its adviser, except to smile now and then at its gravity, and at being still addressed as Acorn when it was so large.

At length the Bucket was seized with terror, with panic ; for it saw the outgrowth of the Acorn becoming larger continually, and concluded that

"It empanelled a jury of tubs, pots, and pans."

some evil power was at work, and some dread event must ensue. So one day, when it had returned to the kitchen in this dismay, it empanelled a jury of tubs, pots, and pans, and accused the Acorn before them. Inasmuch as this Acorn had held no water, it was declared wicked; inasmuch as after being trodden in the earth it had transformed itself to a peculiar shape, it must be demoniac; and as it was growing larger daily, there was a terrible probability that it would ultimately be a monster and devour all of them—Bucket, tubs, pots, and pans—and perhaps even the holy pump itself. A general shudder pervaded the jury; horror was painted on every face; they agreed on a verdict of *guilty*, without leaving their shelves and stands. The Bucket then proceeded to pass sentence of transportation for life upon the Acorn, not, indeed—for it was a well-meaning old Bucket—without a few water-drops of compassion, in advance, for the distress which it must inflict on a fellow-creature.

This sentence the Bucket conveyed and solemnly uttered to the Acorn when it next went to the pump. But the reply came now from a somewhat stout oak-tree.

" Foolish Bucket !" it said ; " it is not for the dead to pass judgment on the living. You who have so long been accustomed to receive whatever is pumped into you, adding nothing to it from yourself, returning to your master every gift un-improved, know that I too have received streams from your venerable pump, and have turned them to inherent strength. By this strength I have become myself a pump, and drawn other wells from the earth, and fountains from the air. While you have received just what was put into you, careless whether it were foul or pure, I have separated the healthful from the harmful, and have also made my every leaf a filter to purify the air for mankind. Those iron bands around you denote that your power to grow has passed away ; you were once alive like me, but now you are dead. When I am dead, they may cut me up into many buckets like you ; but perhaps, if while I am living I grow my best, instead of being made into silly little buckets like you and your kitchen-friends, I may be made a great one, and bear my freight upon the sea."

THE UNFINISHED ISLAND

THE UNFINISHED ISLAND.

IT is an island full of beauty and fruitfulness.
The gently undulating fields are adorned with the
exquisite flowers that circle the year with their
fragrance, and dial the days, weeks, months, with
their opening and closing blossoms. The orchards
are ever laden with fruits, the golden harvests
never fail; the fair island garners every sunbeam
that falls on it in fruits of endless variety. The
terraced shores, always green, slope gently to the
crystal waves of a sea so soft that halcyon seemed
ever brooding over it. This island is inhabited
by a race of gentle islanders, healthy and happy,
who sometime had not been visited by foreign
traders, nor by conquerors, but had been left alone
to develop as much art and civilisation as they
could. They were all devoted to their island-

home ; and they believed that their island had been created by the fairest of all deities in his happiest mood. The tradition was that this fair deity had created it as a place for his own occasional dwelling on earth ; that he had also created a few families who were to dress and tend the island in his absence ; that finally this deity had found reasons to dwell elsewhere, but had entrusted the care of the island to those families, from whom all in the island were descended.

The islanders called their deity the Beautiful One, and they built him a very beautiful temple. Its walls were of marble, and within were tinted arches and pillars of porphyry. Over the altar was a picture of the Beautiful One, as they imagined him, set in a frame of gems. Around the Temple dwelt those who were called the Diviners. It was their office to cultivate and lay fresh flowers daily on the altar, and to compose and sing sweet songs to the Beautiful One.

But of this beautiful island there was one

corner which was wild, chaotic, altogether unlovely. There jagged rocks were interspersed with dark, dank tarns; precipice and pitfall alternated with malarious morass and jungle, in which lurked slimy monsters. For a long time it had been a problem to the natives how the same fair deity that created all that was beautiful in their island could also have made this horrible section of it. But this difficulty had been solved by one of their sages in this way: his explanation was, that the deity in making their island purposely left that bad corner unfinished, as a general challenge to all genii or men who might think they were as able to create beautiful things as himself. If any proud angel or mortal imagined himself equal to the island deity, let him try his hand on that unfinished corner, and prove that he could fashion that to a like beauty with the rest!

The bright Temple stood just on the line which separated the completed from the unfinished part of the island. The Diviners had set upon

its door a tablet, on which were the following
rules :—

THE UNFINISHED CORNER.

In the Name of the Beautiful One :—

It is hereby ordered, in pursuance of revela-
tions received by the Diviners from the Creator
of this Island, that if any mortal be ambitious
enough to try and finish the corner He left in-
complete, such mortal shall be allowed to do so
under the subjoined conditions :—

1. He shall provide himself with as much food
as he can carry with him.

2. After two days his friends may bring food
for him daily, which will be left just outside the
back door of the Temple.

3. He must bring to the Temple, and deposit
as he passes through, one hundred pieces of gold ;
these are to be restored to him with interest when
he returns, his task being completed, but to belong
to the Diviners should he never return.

4. No one shall enter the Unfinished Corner save through the Temple.

5. Only one at a time shall be allowed the attempt to finish the Corner.

For a long time the islanders were so contented and happy with their ample island and its resources, that they rarely occupied their minds with the horrible locality behind the Temple. But they cultivated the Fine Arts chiefly, and gradually their ideas of beauty were so developed that they began to feel unpleasantly the proximity of the dismal region. Occasionally, too, serpents were found creeping beyond the limits of their Corner into the fields where children played; and one was bitten so that he died. Again, several persons were taken down with fevers, and these had an impression that they had been stricken by them while working near the Unfinished Corner.

Although these vague notions and rumours

I

were severely rebuked by the Diviners, who declared it wicked to suppose that their fair deity
had created any region that could injure those
who kept out of it, gradually there arose an Unfinished Corner Reform party. The horrible
chaotic corner became an eyesore, and after a
great deal of discussion, there arose some who,
with no ambition but to serve their fellow-islanders,
took their picks and passed through the Temple.
Not one of these had ever been seen or heard of
again. The relatives and friends of some of them
had desired to make a search for them; but the
Diviners declared that they had a special revelation to prevent that, and they also intimated that
those who had failed in the attempt to finish the
Corner had been transformed into monstrous
creatures. This greatly added to the horrors and
terrors of the Unfinished Corner. It appeared
for a time as if no one would ever again attempt
to finish it, and that the islanders had made up
their minds to endure what could not be cured.

But gradually there grew up in the island a small party who became suspicious of the Diviners. These keepers of the Temple, it was remembered, received a sum of money from every man that passed through, to be restored with interest if he should return, but confiscated if he did not come back—as he never did. So there grew doubts; and finally a number of young men conspired to enter the Unfinished Corner by another way than through the Temple.

At midnight they so entered it, and began their work. They found the rock soft. They cut channels from some tarns and emptied them. Every night, between midnight and daybreak, they toiled, and were rejoiced to perceive that they were making some impression on the chaos. But they grew old. Then they took some of the younger men into their secret, and induced them to carry on the work. As it proceeded, there were found difficult points indeed, some marshes rank with vegetation of ages, some dangerous

serpents that showed a disposition to defend their
slimy abodes, and more that glided away with
fear; nothing insurmountable was met with, no
monster, no demon, not even a wild beast of any
large size.

While the midnight workers found it a very slow
and large task which they had undertaken, they
also recognised more and more the great import-
ance that it should be accomplished. They perceived that the unfinished space was much larger
than the islanders generally knew; that its
improvement would greatly add to their well-
being, wealth, and happiness; and every mind
among them began to find himself sustained and
encouraged in his labours by foreseeing the uni-
versal joy which would fill the island, and fore-
hearing the thanksgivings which would be chanted
in the Temple, when the glad tidings should burst
upon them that the Unfinished Corner existed only
as a part of their fair and completed heritage.

These labours proceeded for a long time unob-

"They had come upon a pit filled up with human bones."

served. Young men were born into the work, and the aged died out of it, for two or three generations. At last one of these companies of midnight workmen, having cut a noble highway up to the back of the pure marble Temple, were just imagining to themselves the joy with which the islanders would presently be greeting their half-triumph over the Unfinished Corner, when lo, a horrible discovery !

They had come upon a pit filled up with human bones.

This, then, had been the fate of the brave pioneers who had dared to try and finish what the Diviners said their deity had left unfinished. They had been cruelly slain, each as he emerged behind the Temple, by those who beguiled the islanders with flowers and music while so robbing them of their best friends.

The labourers who made this discovery returned to announce it. The islanders rushed in a body to the Temple, dragged the Diviners from it; cast them into the pit of their victims, and were about to raze the Temple to the ground when a wise man intervened. By his counsel they gathered up the bones of all who had perished in the attempt to finish the island, and made the Temple their shrine. On it they engraved this legend that I have related, and called it the Reformers' Monument.

Then the islanders plied their hands with a will : rocks were rent and pulverised, tarns drained, marshes and swamps cleared, reptiles exterminated, and at length the once horrible Corner was so fairly finished that only enough of its former ruggedness remained to make it the most picturesque part of the island.

But what became of the deity who was said to have challenged all mortals to equal his work by finishing the island ? Alas! the crimes of his Diviners so deformed that once fair deity, that his name became a byword. The picture of him that had been in the Temple was deprived of its setting of gems, and these were given to the martyrs' families or descendants ; that picture was then set against a wall on the road-side, where the painted eyes might gaze on the work of completing the island. An artist next painted horns on the fair deity's forehead and tusks in his mouth. The natives recognised these as emblems of the wildness his Diviners had tried to preserve in their otherwise perfect little world, and the cruelty with which they had acted. So they put the now grotesque picture in their Island Museum, and wrote beneath it—THIS IS THE FINISHED DEITY OF THE UNFINISHED CORNER.

BOY, CHRYSALIS, AND BUTTERFLY

BOY, CHRYSALIS, AND BUTTERFLY.

A LITTLE boy received as a gift from his mother
a beautiful lily, set in a picturesque pot, which he
cherished with much care. One day he found a
dark streak on a pure petal of one of the flowers,
and on examining it he found that it was a brown,
dirty-looking, seemingly dead worm. When he
tried to brush it off, he found the worm adhering
so closely to the petal that he could not re-
move it without injuring his flower. So he ran
to his mother, and tears stood in his eyes as he
cried, "Mother, there is a naughty, nasty, ugly,
hateful worm on my lily!" The mother went out
with him to see what could be done, but when
they reached the lily the worm could nowhere be
seen. "It's gone!" cried the boy, his eyes full of
surprise. "I'm so glad—but, O mother, do look

at this tiny butterfly which has lit on my flower!
Did you ever see anything so lovely?"

"But that," said the mother, "is that same
creature which you just now called naughty, nasty,
ugly, and hateful. You must have found the
worm just at the moment when it was to become
a butterfly. The poor little thing, ugly as it then
appeared, was fond of your lily, and chose that
pretty spot to find its wings. Hereafter it will
be well to know more of your new acquaintances
before speaking harshly of them; and it is also
well not to judge too much by the outside look of
things, especially not before you are certain they
may not be changing to something else you will
be sorry to have abused."

When his mother had gone into the house, the
Boy, thinking over what she had said, and wonder-
ing at the transformation of the worm, felt even
more interest in this new-born butterfly than in
his lily; he thought that perhaps if he watched it
the pretty creature might go through yet another

"He took it out into the garden and there followed it about."

change and become something still more beautiful. So he placed it in the conservatory among the flowers, where, after a little, it flitted about in delight from blossom to blossom.

But when the Boy came to look at it in the afternoon, it had not changed again, and he took it out into the garden and there followed it about. Something else having attracted his attention for a moment or two, he turned to look for his beautiful butterfly—but it was gone. Alas! now that he knew its story, and his abuse of it as a worm had been followed by admiration, he loved the pretty butterfly; he could not bear to lose it; he searched for it long and long. All in vain! When all hope of finding the beautiful creature again was gone, the Boy sat down on the grass and wept.

Just then his father entering, paused and asked what was the matter. The Boy told him with sobs the tragedy that had happened to him,—the loss of the butterfly. The father laughed, and

K

that seemed cruel till he said," Why, here is the butterfly sitting quietly on your head!"

"And I was looking all over the garden for it!" cried the Boy, as he took it softly into his hand again—laughing through his tears.

"People sometimes look very far for beauty when its wings are folded on their heads," said the father—half to himself.

BULB AND THE MOLECRICKET

THE BULB AND THE MOLECRICKET.

A LITTLE brown Bulb was purchased by a gentle-
man, and planted by his gardener while it was
in a deep sleep, and the first stir of consciousness
in it was a most happy dream. It dreamed
that it was on its way to a beautiful world, spread-
ing above the dark sod in which it lay. Its dust
and ashes were to be left beneath, its ragged brown
clothes to be laid aside for ever ; transformed, nay
transfigured and glorified, it was to ascend to a
splendid palace with a dome of azure, frescoed
with ever-changing many-tinted pictures, and
sometimes lit with innumerable brilliants. The
Bulb dreamed that in that beautiful world its life
would be a pure delight. Surrounded by lovely
sisters and friends, somewhat like itself but just
different enough to make a happy variety, it should

also be visited by higher beings with shining wings
and tuneful voices, and every zephyr should waft
from, as well as to herself, ever fresh sweetness
and joy.

While the Bulb was dreaming this happy dream,
there came by a Molecricket, extending his
gallery, and he paused to speak with his new pa-
rishioner.   He wears a solemn vestment, and the
Bulb confides to him as a holy personage her vision
and longing,—her sweet faith that she will grow
upward to that fair paradise pictured in her dream.

But the Molecricket has a misgiving.   " Suppose," he says, " you have got planted the wrong
way, and should grow downwards ; then you would
go down to a darker dungeon, and the more you
expand, the more wretched you will be,—buried
alive ! "

Then the Molecricket went his way, promis-
ing to return next morning.   He breakfasted on
a beetroot near by, burrowed on with his gallery,
and slept comfortably.

"Suppose you have got planted the wrong way."

He returned as he promised early next morning. Our poor Bulb had passed a wretched day, a miserable night; her dreams had all been of growing downward,—down among worms and noisome things; of being cast away, petal and calyx, unprofitable, into outer darkness! Nay, she had even discovered with horror that she was already growing downwards; she confessed to the solemn Molecricket that she had distinctly felt the downward growths,—several of them,—and cried out in her anguish, "Alas! what can I do, what shall I do, to be saved from the fearful abyss?"

The Molecricket said "he would do his best;" and upon that went at once beneath the Bulb and devoured all the rootlets which it had sent down.

Happy and hopeful, once more our Bulb, touched by the upper warmth, swells and stirs, —but alas! down go the rootlets away from the flowery realm! Again they are eaten away by Molecricket, and yet again; but while thus Molecricket expanded in his region, the poor Bulb expanded not in hers; but wasted away and died. It may be added that when she was dying, her adviser consoled her with a promise of blossoming in another world.

But, alas! the promise was never fulfilled. The owner·of the garden coming to inquire about the flower, learned that it had not appeared. Surprised that a bulb planted so carefully should not have grown in what seemed a favourable season, he ordered the gardener to dig it up. The gardener brought him the shrivelled bulb and said, " Molecrickets have killed it." The master having entered the house expressed some vexation at his rare bulb being killed by molecrickets.

" How did they kill it ?" asked his little daughter.

" By eating off its roots," said the father.

" Can't a thing grow without roots ?"

" What a silly question! Everything must take a good hold on the ground before it can grow up."

" By the way, child," added the father, " I said

you might go to Mrs. Merry's children's party to-
night, but you must not; I hear there is to be
dancing and other worldly amusement. Only last
Sunday you heard that you must not love nor
cling to things earthly, but come out from this
world and its pleasures. Else you would go down
into darkness." The child went away weeping.

Little Emma—that was this child's name—was
indeed sorely disappointed at being forbidden to
go to Mrs. Merry's party. Her mamma had pre-
pared for her a lovely dress for the occasion, but
it had to be put away again, and the pale little
girl sobbed herself to sleep. But at the peep of
day she awoke from a terrible dream. She had
dreamed that she had secretly slipped out of her
bed, put on her fine clothes, and stolen away to
the beautiful ball. She found it as splendid as
that given by the prince in the story of Cinderella.
While she and many other children were dancing
merrily, the clock struck the twelve solemn strokes
of midnight, and immediately they all sank, sank,

down, down, into a dark hole in the middle of the
earth, there buried alive.   She also dreamed—for
what her father said about the bulb and its eaten
roots had stayed in her mind,—that her feet, which
had just now been dancing, put out roots by which
she was held fast, while at the same time all
manner of ugly things were eating those roots,
without, however, setting her free.   Even after
she was awake Emma could not free herself
entirely from the fear which had fallen on her in
this night-vision.   She felt that she must have
had a genuine glimpse into that outer darkness of
which her papa had so solemnly spoken.   And
she now felt thankful to him in her heart for having forbidden her going to Mrs. Merry's party,
and so saved her from the awful calamity which,
she almost expected to hear, had befallen the
dancers during the night.

When she heard next day from her little companions what a beautiful dancing-party they had,
and how they were all in bed and asleep long be-

fore midnight; when she could not find one of those who had been to the dance conscious of having been afterwards buried alive, even in a dream; then Emma began to be perplexed. That night she did not sleep well, but lay awake thinking of all her little companions had told her about the ball and the pretty dresses. Next morning she came down looking very pale, and had no appetite for her breakfast. Emma's mamma was not very anxious that day, but when she found her child continuing pale and peaking, and that, as weeks went on, the roses never came back to her cheek, nor the smiles to her pretty mouth, why then the mother was alarmed. Being a shrewd lady, she also began to suspect that some secret trouble was gnawing at her little girl's heart. So she resolved to find out what was the matter, and kept Emma out of the schoolroom for a morning that she might walk with her in the garden.

"Mamma," said Emma, when they had paused beside a beautiful tulip, "are we like flowers?"

"Like flowers? who?"

"Why, girls—like me."

"What makes you ask?"

"Why, one day papa was holding something in his hand which he said ought to have turned to a flower, but something had eaten off its roots."

"And what has that to do with my little Emma?"

"Papa said everything must get a good hold on the ground with its roots, or it can't grow to a flower. Mamma, have I got any roots, and will they be eaten off?"

The mother's face was burning, and her eyes looked deep into the blue eyes of her little daughter, and searched through all her heart. What she found there made her at once happy and unhappy. She found that little Emma had a sensitive and imaginative nature, a natural eye for beauty everywhere—for beautiful conduct and behaviour in herself and others, as well as beautiful dress and pictures and sports; that she had a heart for joy which ought to make herself and others happy; but she also found, alas! that these powers and dispositions in her little girl were nearly starved. Emma's mamma felt just as if she were a mother-bird who had come to her nest after a long time and found her little birdling's mouth wide open with hunger, but nearly dead because nothing had been put into it.

She made up her own mind as to what ought to be done with Emma, and that is at least half-way towards making up somebody else's mind. She knew that her husband was not only very fond of his flowers, but that he was very wise and scientific about bringing them up; how to bring up children was another thing. Mamma thought she knew more about child-gardening than her dear husband. What, then, should this witty mamma do but go out to the place where the bulb of a favourite flower had been planted by her husband's order, and was already shooting, and practise on it the same kind of gardening as that from which she thought her little girl was suffering.

Presently, by chance she meets Emma's father, and says many things to him, and at last remarks, " I saw just now your fine tulip beginning to shoot."

"Ah! I am so glad of that; the last I planted there died."

" The sunshine was so warm that I covered it over with a tin cup——"

" What ? "

" And, thinking it might have too many roots, I placed near it a molecricket which the gardener had dug up and put in the cup——"

" Why, what have you done?" cried the husband, and away he ran to take the cup from the green shoot, and kill the molecricket.

When he returned he said, " I really could not have believed that a woman of your common sense, after living in a garden so long, would not have known that a flower-shoot needs all the air and sunshine it can get, and that a molecricket is its enemy."

"So," said the wife, " I did for the growing tulip exactly what ought not to have been done for it."

" Exactly."

" Well, forgive me; I'll do better next time, now you have told me. But now let me tell you that I fear you are making the same blunders about a much sweeter and more precious little shoot in our garden."

"Which is it ?"

"Our dear little Emma."

" What's the matter with Emma ? Hasn't she everything she needs ?"

" Maybe; but not all she wants, if you will allow the difference. She has clothing to keep her warm, and food to eat, and a good teacher; but she wants more sunshine, more play and mirth and gaiety; she wants more beauty in her life, pretty dresses, singing and dancing, and bright

L

company.   Now, somehow you have got it into
your mind that these things are wicked, and I fear
that your religion not only covers her with a cup
that shuts out sunshine, but also puts a molecricket
near her roots to eat them away, and prevent her
taking such good hold on the earth as will enable
her to grow to the lovely flower she ought to be."

The tender father and husband felt the truth
of this parable.   He went to his little Emma, who
was moping among the flowers, still pale and perplexed with her dreamy fears, and talked with her.
He found her still fearful about the outer darkness into which he once seemed to think children
might go, and told her he had come to the con-
clusion that there was no danger of that.   He
said he hoped she would be glad and bright as the
flowers were, and the butterflies and the birds.

Before a week had passed, Emma was wearing
her beautiful dress at a little party of her own ;
she danced and played and dreamed a pretty
dream of a charming fancy-ball, in which tulips

and molecrickets waltzed together till midnight, and then all flew up into paradise. The evil shadow of fear never rested again upon her thoughtful mind; play followed study, and amusement joined hands with duty in her life; and so grows Emma to-day with the roses in her cheeks and the violets in her eyes, and with pure thoughts, kind deeds, and gentle words for those around her more sweet and fragrant than any flowers.

THE STREAMLET

THE STREAMLET.

A STREAMLET started forth from a spring in the side of a mountain, and, after an infancy of gay leaps in bright cascades, spread out into a more quiet and steady movement. It began then to dream and meditate on the object for which it existed. While in this grave mood a Will-o'-wisp darted out and danced over its waters.

"Ah," cried the Streamlet, "this is a heavenly light sent to tell me what I wish to know, and to guide my course."

But the Will-o'-wisp soon flitted away and vanished, leaving the Streamlet more perplexed than before. Its first creed was gone. Then a rosy cloud floated in the sky and mirrored itself in the bosom of the Stream.

"This," it cried, "is a token of Paradise!"

But a wind ruffled the water, and the tinted cloud was mirrored no more ; and when the Streamlet became still again, the rosy cloud had passed from the sky.   Then a water-lily expanded on its waves.

"Behold !" said the Streamlet, "to nourish this beauty is the end and aim of my life."

But the lily presently folded up and perished. The Streamlet moved on.   At length it came to a spot where men had thrown hard stones in its way ; these obstructed its course, turned it aside through a narrow channel, and forced it to rush in a confused perilous way over a wheel.

"Alas !" cried the Streamlet ; "is it then for this agony I was born ?"

But after some wild splashes the Streamlet found itself at peace again, and went on widening. And now a glorious moon came out and showered gold all over it.

"How wealthy I am !" cried the Streamlet.

The moon waned.   But the stars came out, and

" So may the stream of my life run on."

the ripples caught them as bright marvels ; they hinted deeper, steadier glories yet to be revealed. But the stars set.

At length a poet reclined on its banks and sang to it :

"Sweet Streamlet! What a bright life must have been yours ! What flowers must have fringed your gliding way, what rosy clouds you have reflected, what lilies you have nourished, what stars have risen to tell you their secrets ere they have set! You have done brave work, too. You have watered the meadow and made it wave with grain ; you have conspired with the sun to ripen the harvest, and when matured you have helped to turn it into bread. Not for any one of these joys and uses were you made, but for all ! So may the stream of my life run on, with varied happiness and helpfulness, not anxious about the unknown Sea to which thou and I, fair Stream, are tending."

As the Streamlet listened, all the beauties it

had known shone out again, and they all clustered
—dancing light, rosy cloud, lily, golden moon and
serene stars—around the great sorrow it had encountered, the obstruction which had ground grain
for man ; for that, transfigured in the Poet's song,
seemed the happiest experience of all.

THE CHILD AND THE IMAGE

"She hid her face in her mother's skirt."

THE CHILD AND THE IMAGE.

A LITTLE girl was taken by her parents to visit an
ancient cathedral. While the parents were admir-
ing some fine old traceries about the door, they
were startled by a piercing cry from their child,
who shrank from the portal with signs of terror,
and hid her face in the mother's skirt.

"What is the matter?" cried both parents at
once.

"Oh, the ugly man up there!" gasped the girl.
"O mother, he has horrible horns and teeth,
I'm afraid of him." And the little one shuddered.

The father's eye caught in a moment the figure
which had so terrified his little daughter. On one
side of the portal was a sculptured mediæval figure
with horns and pitchfork, and large tusks; a fiend-
ish grin of malicious delight was on his face as he

M

trampled men and women down into a monster's
mouth yawning at his feet. The father half
smiled at his child's dismay, and said :—

"Do not fear, my darling. It cannot hurt you ;
it is only stone ; we won't look at it any more, but
go into the church." And he took her hand.

"Oh no, no !" cried the Child, still cowering,
and again clasping her mother. "He's inside the
church ; I know he is. Let's run away !"

"He's not inside," said the father ; "there are
beautiful forms within. Don't be afraid."

"But why do they put him there ?" asked the
girl, peeping out at the figure from the folds of her
mother's dress.

"They placed him there when the church was
built, hundreds of years ago."

"Who did ?"

"The men who built the church."

"They must have been very naughty men, and
I don't love them at all," said the Child.

The parents were now laughing heartily, and

the girl, reassured by their merriment, looked up again at the figure.

" Is it funny ?" she said.

" No," said the father ; " but it is funny that . you should be frightened at such an old Image, which can only make grown-up people smile, or look at it as a curiosity."

" What is a curiosity ?" said the Child.

" Something queer,—not like what you see every day."

The Child was still puzzled.

" Did children put it there for grown-up people to laugh at ?" she inquired.

" Well, my little one, you see, the whole world was something like a child once. Can you understand that ?"

" Not a bit," sighed the girl.

" I mean that, a long time ago, people, even after they were grown up, used to be frightened at big black clouds, and lightning, and at the dark, just as you were frightened by that stone."

" I am not afraid of the dark," said the Child.

"No; because your mother and I, and all your friends, were never afraid of it; nor of clouds and thunder. But when the world was a child, as I told you, it had not found out what darkness is, and what the clouds are made of. Then they thought that the cloud and thunder and the dark and everything ugly, and everything they were afraid of,—snakes and tigers and cruel men,— must have been made by a bad deity—not the same that made the blue sky and the roses. Now, that ugly figure there is that bad deity."

"Oh, oh!" exclaimed the Child, "I'm afraid of him! Where does that bad one live?"

"He doesn't live at all. There isn't any bad deity. They thought so, but they were mistaken, —just as you were mistaken in thinking that stone could hurt you."

"But why did they not take it down when they found they were mistaken?"

"Why, when they found that the clouds and darkness and snakes and tigers were not made by any bad power, they still thought there must be one, because there were so many bad men and women. When people killed each other, and did other wicked things, they thought there must be a big wicked creature who made them do it, in order that he might get them after they were dead, and treat them cruelly. So they kept him up there to make people believe how ugly it was to be wicked and cruel, and what a horrible monster would get them."

"But didn't it frighten good people? How could people play with their dolls and eat cake if they thought there was a bad one with horns and great teeth to eat everybody he could?"

"Well, yes, it did frighten good people, till they rose above it."

"Father, what *do* you mean by *rose above it?*"

"O dear little questioner, we must really go on now, and talk about all this at another time. I mean that they rose above it by finding that there was not really any such monster, just as you rose above your fear when we told you the figure could not hurt you."

The three entered the cathedral. The parents pointed out to their child a beautiful statue of the Madonna, but the Child said, softly :

" Mother, if that ugly one with horns were alive, I could never play with my dolly. I would hide her."

" Don't think of that any more, little daughter," said the mother ; "look at that beautiful babe with light around its head, on the gay-coloured window."

The Child gazed, but was silent ; the cloud had not lifted. Presently, they passed up a winding stair-way, and stepped forth upon a parapet beneath the clear morning sky. Then the mother saw that her darling's eyes were full of tears. She pressed the Child to her breast, and soothed her, and pointed her to the brilliant city.

Soon after, the Child, grasped by her father's hand, was suffered to look over the parapet's edge, and, after gazing for a minute, she uttered another cry,—this time a cry of delight.

"Mother, mother, only see! here, just below us

on the wall, is a nest and four dear little birds, and there is an egg, too, quite sky-blue! What a cozy place they have ; it's just made for a nest."

The mother hastened to look, and even while the two were gazing on the little family, the mother-bird came, and the father-bird, and there were happy twitterings. The Child's delight was great. But the mother's eye had observed something else, and she said :

" Why, my darling, that place you think so cozy for a nest is exactly on the top of the head of the ugly Image that troubled you so ! See, his horns keep it from falling. The mother-bird isn't fright-ened, but nestles on them ! "

" Why, so it is !" exclaimed the little one. " The bad man doesn't look ugly from here; his head holds up the bird's nest."

" That," said the father, "may show just what I meant when I told you that people rose above it. You are now above it. When you looked up to it, it was frightful : when you look down on it, you can see something sweet and loving going on over

it, and even held up by it.   And some day, when
you have grown larger, you shall love to remember
to-day, and how you came to look down on the
demon the first day you ever saw him."

"Come, father and mother!" cried the happy
Child.   "The little boys and girls downstairs may
be frightened; let us go and stand in the church-
door, and tell them not to look at the demon there,
where he's horrid, but to come up here and see,
over his horns, the sky-blue egg, and the mother-
bird feeding its young."

The tears had disappeared from the Child's
eyes, but they stood bright in those of the parents.

THE DEWDROP

" To gaze upon the sea, which was near the humble cottage."

THE DEWDROP.

A LITTLE boy, whose parents were very poor, suffered from an accident, by which he was lamed for life, and his health sadly impaired. But his mind was active, and his disposition gentle and cheerful. He loved nature, and every day, aided by his crutch, went to walk along the cliffs and gather flowers, to listen to the language of birds, or to gaze upon the sea, which was near the humble cottage. The parents had long known the wonderful intelligence and sweet nature of their little invalid, and it cut them to the heart that they had not the means of securing for him the education which his faculties needed. Unable to labour as he was, the boy's lot seemed to be only that of adding to his parents' toil and poverty; and as he grew older, the perception of this threw a shade over his naturally cheerful spirit. He longed for books, but they could not be obtained; and while the scenes of nature charmed him, gradually even the sky and blue sea, the bright clouds above and snowy sails beneath, became shadowed from the gathering gloom upon his heart. The sea seemed to be assuming a sterner line, the flowers appeared to fold up more and more, and the birds' voices, which he once thought he understood, were beginning to sound as if they no longer meant anything for him. The poor boy's walks were continued, but they became sadder, and he did not carry back from them so many flowers and sunbeams as formerly, in his heart and eyes, to gladden the humble cottage. Nay, he brought back a heavy heart, which said to itself, " My life must for ever be wasted : all the beauty that the sky has shed upon my thoughts has led them forth only to wither; all the sweet secrets which the flowers have told me are turning to thorns !"

On the side of a cliff near which the boy sometimes walked, and on top of which was a peculiar stone on which he used to sit—trying to decipher some scratches on it, which he thought had been made by human hands—there grew a wild columbine. On this columbine there gathered one evening a Dewdrop. "What a superb flower is this to which I have come!" thought the crystal droplet. The blue had not yet faded out of the sky; it touched, with a soft tint, the little drop, which looked up until it presently caught the glory of the evening star. With these colours playing through it the Dewdrop was happy enough, but the joy did not last. Evaporation began; a strange presentiment of danger, then a sense of weakness, came over the bright droplet, and at the same time the shadows deepened in the sky, and the colour of the columbine was dulled. The Dewdrop was now heavy-hearted, and it said, " My life must for ever be wasted : all the beauty that the sky shed on me has kindled hopes only to wither them ; all the love that my flower inspired is turning to pain!"

Just then a gentle wind came and shook the columbine, and the Dewdrop fell on a bit of limestone ; its brief life, that opened so beautiful, had ended in a speck of moisture on a speck of rock. Into a vein of the limestone fragment the Dewdrop sank, and lay there as in its tomb. In the gray of morning a frosty breath came, and the vein of moisture, which had once been a Dewdrop, was changed to ice. When the sun rose a breath of warmth passed over the icy form and expanded it, and though the force of the expansion was small, a little cleft was left in the stone, as from its tomb the spirit of the Dewdrop exhaled.

The processes of nature are often through agencies small in themselves, large in functions. This little rift in a fragment of rock, made by the thaw of a little frost—the fallen Dewdrop,—was the last of a large number of influences which had preceded it. The force of gravitation, which had been pulling at that fragment of limestone for a long time, now succeeded in casting down a bit of the under side so loosened. Very slight was this change, but it left the rest of the fragment too weak to support a mass of gravel that lay upon it. That, too, gave way, and a slight landslide followed. This undermined a larger rock, which fell, and the movement so begun did not end till it had reached the top of the cliff.

On the day after all this had happened at the cliff our invalid boy went on his accustomed walk, to study the only book he had—nature,—and at length reached the point where he had been wont to rest. But a part of the path had fallen, and with it the stone with its peculiar marks, which had often amused him as he sat upon it. But what was this that caught his eye? On the very edge of the precipice was a casket. The boy could not reach it with his arm, but his crutch served him, and he soon had it in his hands. It was filled with rare and precious gems. It was not in a country where treasure-trove could be taken from the finder; the jewels were ancient, and their owner was called for in vain.

The lame boy carried back that day not mere wealth, but culture and greatness. Far and wide through the world are his thoughts now winging their way, bearing the priceless jewels of courage and hope to hearts that else had been wasted. What work he had done, and for whom, he knew as little as the Dewdrop perishing in its grief, dreaming not that its little life and death would enrich the world. The pious mother believed that an angel had brought from paradise the casket which her dear invalid had found ; and in sooth it *was* something like an angel, that pure Dewdrop softly distilled from the sky, softly ascending ; bearing with it mighty forces, itself traceable only in transformations.

A PRETTY CUSTOM

A PRETTY CUSTOM.

THE city of Bithar, according to some Eastern traditions, was once the largest and most brilliant in the world. Ancient rabbins have told many legends about it, and on one of these is based the following story; but I believe this will be found (should the matter ever be searched into by historians) the only true and full account of Bithar.

It was, then, a beautiful city. Its palaces, temples, and theatres were built of many-coloured marbles, and decorated with every ornament that public wealth and cunning workmanship could bestow. Grand also were the mansions of the citizens, who numbered half a million. The fine and useful arts of these inhabitants, their commerce and general enterprise, combined with the exceeding great bounty of nature and healthiness of climate, had banished poverty and the many vices to which it tempts mankind. So flourished Bithar for some centuries, insomuch that foreigners who wandered there invented fine phrases in which to express their admiration. Some called it "The Opal City," others "The Earth's Coronet," and often it was named "The Beautiful."

Now this happy people of Bithar had among them what was called "a pretty custom," and no doubt some of my young readers will also say it was a very pretty custom. It was this: in the grave of every person that died, young or old, an evergreen tree was planted. This was the only kind of tomb, if it can be so called, known in Bithar. Each family kept at home a book in which the names of those who died were recorded, with a suitable account of their lives, and an exact note of the point at which they were buried, and their tree planted, in the Evergreen Cemetery. The trees were planted quite young; each family watered, pruned, and tended carefully every such memorial of its dead ; and it was handed down as a sacred trust, from generation to generation, in every household, to cherish the evergreens of its ancestors.

In the course of time the city of Bithar was completely encircled by a vast forest of ever-greens, emblems of never-fading life without any signs of death among them. This wondrous grove became almost the chief pride and delight of the citizens. Under the Prince of Bithar, the First Minister was he whose special office it was to guard and inspect this flourishing cemetery, to warn families if any of their trees needed more care, and to report on the growth of the trees, some of which gradually reached a vast size.

Early in the history of this wonderful city there had arisen poets, who celebrated in charm-ing verses the green grove. And after some generations there arose minstrels, who set the poets' ballads to music and sang them. When-ever one had died in any house, and just after the

burial, these minstrels came before the door of
the mourning household and sang these songs,
choosing the ballads which were most soothing
and full of hope.

The popularity of these songs led the writers
of Bithar to vie with each other as to which could
write the prettiest praises of the evergreens. But
when all had been written, and said, and sung,
that any one could fancy or imagine about the
evergreens in general, the poets began to fix upon
certain particular trees, and mark their peculi-
arities, their differences from others either in their
shape, size, or shades of green.

A man appeared at Bithar from some far
country, whose name was Suleiman. He was a
man of much learning, of noble presence, and
gracious manner ; and the citizens welcomed him.
He dwelt at Bithar for a long time as a teacher ;
and among the many new doctrines which he
taught there was one concerning the evergreens
which greatly interested the citizens. He called

their attention to the fact that while some of the
evergreens grew large and stately and flourished,
others were weaker, and perhaps gnarled, some
hardly more than dwarfs. There must be a cause
for this ; and Suleiman suggested that these trees
revealed the moral nature of the persons buried
beneath them. This idea spread through all
minds : it became an accepted belief that if any
tree rose higher than others around it, it was because of some profound virtue in the person there
buried; while if any evergreen was feeble, dwarfed,
or unshapely, it was supposed to be due to some
fault or sin which, though it might have been kept
secret during life, was thus made known after death.

After Suleiman's time there was some division
among the people of Bithar about this doctrine of
his ; for now and then evergreens planted above
persons much loved in life turned out poorly, and
the friends of these were troubled that they should
be suspected of being bad-hearted because their
trees were. Yet, Suleiman's name carried even

more weight after his death than during his life, and his doctrine continued to be generally believed.

In the next generation after Suleiman there came to Bithar from another distant region (a country remote from that whence Suleiman had come) a great man named Karitása. He also remained there as a sage of high renown, and he too taught the people a new doctrine concerning their evergreens. This was, that these trees were mysteriously connected with the souls of persons buried beneath them; and that good things poured about the roots of these trees, such as perfumed waters or liquids agreeable to the taste, would be enjoyed by those supposed to be dead, but really alive.

This doctrine was no sooner universally accepted than it found many things to confirm it. Some persons walking amid the evergreens could hear soft whispered words stirring amid their branches; the more fanciful could sometimes even hear what one tree said to another. Others, again, saw now and then lights glancing amid the dark boughs—especially when they walked through the grove by moonlight. There thus grew up amid the evergreens many legends, fables, strange stories, which became confirmed traditions and flourished as much as the trees.

Thus, at the time when there occurred the startling events I am about to relate, it had become the general religious faith of the people of Bithar that every evergreen was the house and home of a soul; that this explained why evergreens were not subject to annual blight of foliage like other trees; that in keeping an evergreen in good condition they were keeping a departed soul in good condition; and that if any evil happened to its tree a soul suffered pain. It was even believed that the very immortality of every soul depended upon its tree; for every tree that perished, a soul perished utterly and for ever!

One cannot wonder then, that as time went on, the people of Bithar took increasing care of this

great green cemetery, which had become to them
a sacred grove in which their departed friends
lived and walked invisibly, and enjoyed themselves. The forest had many guardians.

It came to pass that a fair princess,—she was
little more than a girl,—was once journeying along
the high road near Bithar. She was her royal
father's only daughter, and he loved her so that
he could hardly be persuaded to part with her for
even a little time. But he had consented, because
his dear Leila,—that was her name,—had so longed
for it, to let her go on a visit to a brother of his,
and pass a few weeks with her young cousins.
This well-beloved little princess, confided to the
king's trustiest servants, started off in her chariot,
full of happiness.

Some days and nights were required for the
journey. It was a delightful change for the
princess. At intervals during the day the caval-
cade paused, and a banquet was spread beneath
the shade of some ancient tree; when night came,

a beautiful tent was set up, and, while sentinels stood around, the little princess slumbered serenely among her watchful maids.

On a fair day, when this happy company was passing along a highway unknown to any of them, an accident occurred : the axle-tree of Leila's chariot broke. There was no danger ; the princess easily alighted, and the mechanics who travelled in her retinue at once made preparations to repair the chariot. For this, however, a tree had to be felled, and one of the servants who went to cut one that would make a good axle soon found a cedar which he thought would answer the purpose exactly.

Alas! he little knew what he was doing. The cedar he had chosen was one of the holy trees of Bithar. When his axe was heard, the guardians of the evergreens hastened towards the spot whence the strange sound proceeded. The tree was cut about one-third through when the fore-most keeper arrived, and sprang upon the wood-

cutter, who, in his astonishment, had let fall his
axe. The two men now struggled together, each
calling aloud to his comrades for help. The two
parties ran forward, but the forest-guardians were
strongest, and the servant-men overpowered,
several of them being slain. The chief attendant
of the princess lifted her swooning form to his
saddle and fled with her, not knowing what
danger was behind.

It was a two days' journey back to the palace
of Leila's father. The tents and food had been
left with the chariot, and the faithful attendant,
who had to carry the princess all that way, was
compelled to beg for her food by day, and shelter
at night, from humble peasants along the road.
Leila had, indeed, speedily recovered from her
swoon and first fright; she kept up her courage,
and only lamented that her visit to her uncle and
cousins had been spoiled. But when she had
arrived at the palace of her father, the little princess was taken very ill, through the fright,

exposure, and fatigue ; her life was for a time in danger, and it was a month before she had fully recovered.

The King was extremely angry at this event, and, having called together his Council, it was resolved that redress should be sought with the sword. The people approved of this. " It is not to be endured," they said, " that the highways of the world should be infested by savages so very brutal that they not only attack peaceful travellers, but murder them in the moment of their distress, when common humanity would have rendered aid. This outrage had no excuse whatever,"—so said the people; and it was generally understood among them that the wretches of Bithar meant to seize their lovely princess as a prize for their prince.

While this was being said in one region, a scene was occurring at Bithar. The family, one of whose ancestors was represented by the cut tree, healed up the wound of the evergreen with tenderest care, and rewarded the guardian who had saved it from destruction. They then gathered all their connections together, and held a thanksgiving-day in the chief temple, in honour of the rescue of the soul of their ancestor from death at the hands of barbarians. Some of the citizens of Bithar thought that the party driven off must have been ghouls in human guise, hungry for their dead friends, and unable to reach them except by cutting down their evergreens. They set a larger guard among the trees. "It is not to be endured," said they, "that our highways should be infested by savages so very brutal that they seek to destroy the very souls of our departed relatives. This outrage had no excuse whatever,"—so said the people of Bithar.

The story of a generation may be summed in a sentence. There followed thirty years of skirmishes and struggles, ending in the great siege of Bithar, which effaced it from the earth, and scattered through many lands all who survived of its half-million inhabitants.

" There is now only a silent forest of evergreens. "

Where the wondrous city stood there is now only a silent forest of evergreens, idly and endlessly propagating themselves. In the centre is a monument on which are engraved these words :— THIS IS THE CITY OF THE DEAD, WHO, KEPT ALIVE BY A PRETTY CUSTOM, LAID IN RUINS THE CITY OF THE LIVING.

THE PROCESSION OF UNKNOWN
POWERS

THE PROCESSION OF UNKNOWN POWERS.[1]

A YOUTH went forth in the morning twilight and sat on a summit of a hill, gazing upon the still slumbering villages below. While he sat there a weird procession passed before him. Out of the region of shadows they came, into the same they passed from their vast circuit; and between dusk and dusk their tall swarthy forms were revealed in full outline by the flaming star which each bore with an uplifted hand. The other hand of each was bent with open palm earthward. Though their faces were stern, yet were they beautiful; but though the youth longed that their eyes should turn towards him and some word fall from their lips, silently they passed on, each with eyes

[1] Suggested by one of the last designs of the late David Scott.

bent forward on the vacancy. He spoke, but they heeded not; he shouted, but they responded not; at last he wept and implored, and stretched toward them pleading hands, but they returned him no sign.

At length the sun rose; its splendour shot over the earth, and nothing could be seen but light columns of rose-tinged cloud. From these the youth turned and hastened homeward; through the day he sat dreaming of his vision, and in the night he could not rest. Ere the daybreak he sat again on the summit, and to his great joy the procession of genii again appeared. This time, he thought, they will surely speak to me; or, at least, they will pause and alight upon the earth, or give me some sign of the errand on which they are bound. But it was not so: still their feet touched not the earth, no star was lowered, nor eye bent downward; the plaintive cries of the youth gained no response, and the morning light again smote the wondrous forms into floating mist.

"Stretched toward them pleading hands, but they returned him no sign."

Day after day, as it was breaking, found the youth speeding from his feverish couch ; as its bright hours passed, saw him tranced in gloomy abstraction ; and the night brought out its stars only that they might be eclipsed by the upheld flames of his phantoms. So glided by the weeks into months, and the months into years, and the whole heart and life of the youth were gone out into pallor and pain, as he thought only of the incomprehensible forms. With them went out the sweet hopes and joys of those around him. Parent and brother, sister and lover, waited and watched for the return of his affection and interest in vain.

One day, when he had come from his watch, it was told him that one who had formerly shared his love lay dying. A shudder, as if some glimmer of a bright world now dead had struggled painfully through the cloud that cloaked him, passed through his frame for an instant, but the next moment saw him still as if turned to stone.

But in the night that loved one seemed to stand beside him, and said,—" Since thou didst die to me in the land of the living, let me live to thee in the world of the dead. A shape in thy home, thou meetest me in this abode to which thou hast preceded me, but bringing the darkness of thy senses with thee. Thou longest to know the meaning of the phantoms, and of the stars they bear. Listen ! Their names are Life, Pain, Thought, Love, Death. The mystical stars they bear mean that, starlike, they follow their courses, unhasting, unresting, never swerving. Their steadfast eyes bend not to thee, and their ears are deaf to thy cries, because they exist only in their eternal purpose. One sign alone they had for thee, which, alas, thou couldst not understand— the hand stretched downward. That would have said, ' As we pass steadfastly on our orbits, bear each our appointed star, fulfilling the task ordained, even so do thou on earth, though thy star be a brief love, thy task a child's happiness.' Whilst thou hast vainly pleaded to know the secret of Life, its reality was with the butterfly that alighted on thy shoulder, and the flower that opened beside thee unheeded. Whilst thou wert pondering the mystery of Pain, thou hast not cared that it was piercing hearts around thee. Whilst dreaming of the source of Thought, thoughtless hast thou been; speculating about Love, thou hast shut it out from its nest in thy heart; and grasping after the meaning of Death, thou hast made it the fearful guest of thy home."

In the gray morning the youth awakened from his dream. He thought not of the phantoms, but only of the dear face that had bent over him, and the voice that had spoken sad words. Thenceforth beside that bed over which Death was hovering he sat till he saw the tide of life returning, and lo, when health and joy glowed there again, he saw the face of one of the phantoms as if turned from its star-path to befriend him! The youth made hearts forget their pain in his songs; his winged

hand achieved sublime works for men ; he knew
the morning in tints of the petal and the shell ;
the unswerving stars answered him in beaming
eyes, and the lips of the genii as they passed
kissed as a lover him who had risen to their path
by travelling his own with a steadfastness equal to
theirs.